Susannah and the Blue House Mystery

Susannah and the Blue House Mystery

by Patricia Elmore

illustrated by John C. Wallner

E. P. DUTTON · NEW YORK

Library of Congress Cataloging in Publication Data

Elmore, Patricia.   Susannah and the Blue House mystery.

SUMMARY: After the death of the kindly old man who
lives in a blue house, a girl and her friends attempt
to piece elusive clues together in hopes of finding a
treasure they think he has left to one of them.
[1. Inheritance and succession—Fiction.   2. Mystery and
detective stories]   I. Wallner, John C.   II. Title.
PZ7.E4796Su   1980   [Fic]   79-20491   ISBN: 0-525-40525-9

Published in the United States by E. P. Dutton, a Division
of Elsevier-Dutton Publishing Company, Inc., New York

Published simultaneously in Canada by Clarke,
Irwin & Company Limited, Toronto and Vancouver

Editor: Ann Durell   Designer: Claire Counihan

Printed in the U.S.A.
10 9 8 7 6 5 4 3

to my talented and understanding parents
Winona and Thomas Henry Elmore
for their love and encouragement

One

ONCE OR TWICE a week Susannah Higgins and I stopped on our way home from school to visit her precious Beelzebub. Susannah was an amateur herpetologist, as she put it. As I put it, she was a snake freak, and Beelzebub was about the most repulsive specimen you'd ever hope not to meet. The pet shop owner always greeted us eagerly, hoping Susannah's grandmother had finally agreed to let her buy him. But Susannah's grandmother wasn't nuts.

Beelzebub doesn't have anything to do with the mystery except that the pet store was two blocks from the Blue House, as we came to call it. And that's why we'd gotten off the bus at that particular corner that Friday afternoon and beat it into the pet store before Knievel Jones, my sworn enemy, could start something.

When we came out, Knievel was gone, but Juliet Travis was still standing at the bus stop, where she'd gotten off with us twenty minutes ago.

"Grandpa hasn't come," she fretted, fingering the burn scar that covered one side of her face.

I was surprised she even spoke to us until I remembered that Susannah is one of the few people at school Juliet does talk to. Susannah thinks Juliet is so shy because back in the lower grades kids made fun of her scar. Little kids don't know any better.

"Don't worry," said Susannah. "Your grandpa probably forgot the time."

Juliet shook her head. "Grandpa never forgets. Not even when it rains."

That was true. Every day since I could remember, the shaggy-haired old man in the patched overcoat was always waiting at that bus stop. I noticed because that's the stop where we get rid of Knievel Jones and I can quit worrying about getting a spitball in the neck or worse. I'd wondered what a scruffy old tramp was doing meeting Juliet. I also wondered how he'd come by a cane with a silver handle.

Juliet looked ready to cry. Susannah took her arm.

"We'll walk home with you, won't we, Lucy? Your grandpa will be there, you'll see. Bet his clock stopped." But I caught a look of curiosity on Susannah's dark face. She was always looking for a mystery, ever since the day she'd invited me to be her partner in detective work. But so far we were detectives with nothing to solve. And this certainly didn't look to me like the start of any great mystery.

That was how we first came to see the Blue House up close. We'd noticed it from the bus many times. Even with all the funny old houses in this part of California, this one stood out. Perched on a rise above its newer neighbors, the balcony sagging and the tower windows boarded up, the faded blue paint peeling, still it must have been a mansion in its day.

"Why, this is the old Withers house!" Susannah exclaimed as Juliet opened the rusty iron gate. I might have known she'd learned something about it. "My grandmother remembers when it was one of the finest houses around, back when the Withers family were about the richest people in northern California."

A proud smile flickered over Juliet's tense face. "Grandpa's the last of the Withers. Of course," she sighed, "he's not rich anymore."

"You live *here*?" I couldn't believe anybody our age ever played in that overgrown yard.

"Uh-uh, next door." Juliet gestured over the hedge toward a small, run-down apartment house. Without waiting for more questions, she ran up the cracked walk to the front porch.

The porch groaned as we crossed it. Up close, I saw a shutter hanging crookedly, clinging to a last rusted hinge.

We pounded the door and called. There was no answer.

"The shades are down," I pointed out as we walked around to the back of the house, knocking on windows and yelling as we went.

"They always are," Juliet said. "Grandpa likes it that way. He sits on the porch or in the garden most of the day."

The "garden," I gathered, was the mass of weeds around two trees and an ancient birdbath.

We beat on the back door until even Juliet gave up. She led us through the hedge to her apartment.

Juliet's place was as messy as ours gets before Pop goes on a cleaning binge or his latest lady-friend straightens things up. The dishes in the sink and the piles of books and clothes on the kitchen table looked like home, so Juliet needn't have apologized.

"Mom doesn't have much time to clean up." She blushed and rubbed her burn-scarred cheek. "She paints, you know."

Then she forgot her embarrassment and pushed through the dining room door, calling, "Mom, have you seen Grandpa?"

"Juliet, where have you been? You promised to come straight home and do the laundry." In the clutter of newspapers, boxes, paint tubes and dirty dishes stood an easel and a woman in paint-spattered jeans. "Never mind. Just make me a cup of tea, will you,

5

dear? Oh hello," she added, noticing Susannah and me.

"Mom," Juliet's voice cut through our hellos. "Have you seen Grandpa?"

"Why no, sweetheart. Who are your friends? Come here, dear. What fine bone structure." Taking Susannah's chin, Mrs. Travis slowly turned her head back and forth. "And those eyes . . . like an African princess. I must sketch—"

"Mom!" Juliet's voice was shrill. "Grandpa didn't meet my bus, and he doesn't answer the door. Please think, Mom. Did Grandpa go anywhere?"

"No, dear, you know he never does." Still gazing at Susannah, Mrs. Travis picked up her sketch pad and pencil, then paused. "Oh yes, I think he did say he was going somewhere special when he dropped by for coffee after seeing you off this morning. Didn't say where, though, just that he'd be back in time to meet your bus."

"Mom, I told you. He didn't come."

"I wouldn't worry," Mrs. Travis murmured, removing Susannah's glasses and pulling her closer to the light. "Mr. Withers probably got to talking to Joe and forgot the time."

"Joe? He went to see Joe? Well, why didn't you say so?" Juliet's shoulders relaxed.

"He must have. Where else would he go? And I'm sure he said something about seeing Joe. Though why he asked to borrow the umbrella when there wasn't a sign of rain—" Mrs. Travis rubbed her pencil against her chin, frowning, then brightened. "Quit worrying. He'll be back soon. Meantime let's have a party for your friends."

Frankly I've seen better parties. The only eats Juliet could scrounge up were limp graham crackers and a jar of honey, and alfalfa mint tea to wash them down.

Mrs. Travis chattered on as we ate, covering Juliet's fidgety silence. "I'm so glad Juliet's made some nice friends at last. Didn't I tell you, sweetie? Juliet's so shy," she sighed as Juliet reddened and turned away. "She thinks her burn scar makes her ugly. Never mind, dear, one of these days we'll have enough money for the operation to remove it. You just wait and see." But she didn't sound too sure.

"You suppose we ought to call the police?" Juliet asked as it got to be four-thirty.

"First, why don't you call his friend Joe?" Susannah asked. I'd been wondering that myself. "You said Mr. Withers might be with him, didn't you, Mrs. Travis?"

"Yes," she said, "but I don't know who Joe is. Mr. Withers has never told us."

I was beginning to think Mrs. Travis didn't know much about her own father—for I supposed Mr. Withers must be her father if he was Juliet's grandfather—when she set us straight.

"Mr. Withers isn't really related to us, you understand. He and Juliet just like to pretend he's her grandfather. It's nice for him because he doesn't have any relatives except for a niece, Ivy Withers, whom he hardly ever sees. Juliet needs a grandfather, too, especially since she's never known her father. We got divorced when she was still a baby."

We tried to cheer up Juliet before we left, saying Mr. Withers would be home by suppertime. But he wasn't.

I'd hardly started my breakfast the next morning, a Saturday, when Susannah phoned. "Mr. Withers didn't come home last night. They've phoned the police. I told Juliet we'd come right over."

Two

FUNNY HOW Susannah and I ever became partners. Not so long ago I was about the last person she was thinking of for the detective agency she planned. As for me, I thought of Susannah as my second-worst enemy after Knievel Jones.

Not that Susannah tripped me or stuck Kick Me signs on my rump like Knievel Jones, but she was always nagging me about forgetting my homework or flunking spelling tests. And just let me shoot one tiny rubber band at Knievel—you'd have thought I'd tossed a bomb into the middle of the classroom. Granted, Susannah was the captain of our group, and okay, so the only time our group won the Top Scholars Award was the week I was home with a broken wrist. I didn't see that gave her any right to call me a "dumb blonde" or to groan to the teacher: "Do I *have* to have this clown in my group? I wouldn't mind so much if she really was as dumb as she acts, but—"

I made no secret of the way I felt about Susannah either. I still have cartoons I drew of her then, peering over her glasses at her math book, her forehead rumpled in thought as she twisted one of the twin clumps of curly black hair on her neck.

The cartoons didn't seem to bother her, but something I whispered to the girl who sat between us in class did. And on the bus home that day, she had it out with me.

"What do you mean telling Gail I'm a liar?" Susannah plunked herself and an armload of books on the seat beside me.

"I never said that," I protested, but I couldn't help inching closer to the window. I'd never seen Susannah Higgins so angry before. "I only said you act like you know everything and think you're so important. You *prevaricate*—well, you *do*. Remember, that was one of our vocabulary words."

To my astonishment, Susannah burst into laughter. "That word was *pontificate,* you idiot. *Prevaricate* means to tell lies. You didn't mean I tell lies, you meant I act like—" She paused, thinking it over, then gulped. "You mean—you mean—oh . . ." Her grin faded.

"I sure do," I said grimly. "I mean you act like you know everything. And I mean *everything.*"

Her eyebrows scrunched together over her glasses, then arched out at me. "Yeah, I suppose I do pontificate at times. Sorry."

I think that was the moment I began to like Susannah Higgins. Maybe that was when she also began to like me.

So here on a foggy California Saturday morning in October, Susannah had at last found a mystery to solve: Where was Mr. Withers?

I jammed a pancake into my mouth and took off for Juliet's.

Susannah was already there and Mrs. Travis, her breezy manner gone, was drinking cup after cup of a peculiar-smelling brew. "Chamomile, plantain and mugwort with rose hips," she said. "Very calming to the nerves." But judging from the way she paced the floor, I wasn't convinced. Juliet smiled sadly at us and went back to gazing out the window.

"The police haven't located him yet," said Mrs. Travis, "and we've called the hospitals. He has a bad heart, you know. Of course, he'll probably come strolling up any minute." She tried to laugh, but it didn't work.

"Interesting." Susannah pushed up her glasses, which promptly slid down her nose again. "And you're quite sure you can't remember anything about this Joe? His last name or where he works or—"

11

Mrs. Travis and Juliet shook their heads. "Grandpa never told us," Juliet said.

"Anybody else he might have gone to see?" Susannah asked.

Mrs. Travis shook her head. "He hasn't any other friends that I know of. There's his niece Ivy, of course. I tried to call her, but her answering service said she was out of town. I doubt she'd know where he is, anyway."

"Ivy Withers!" Susannah snapped her fingers. "I think my grandmother knows her. Isn't she the president of the Literary Society and the Concert Guild and just about everything else? Wow, imagine her having an uncle like—I mean—" She looked embarrassed.

"I know what you mean." Mrs. Travis smiled. "I doubt Ivy tells many of her *important* friends about him. She certainly doesn't show him off at those big parties she gives."

Susannah stood up. "Well, we can't do anything sitting here. I think it's time we took a look in the Blue House."

"But I told you, I checked the house before I called the police." Mrs. Travis's voice was shrill. "I have a key, you know, because I clean for him on Tuesdays. Ivy pays me."

Odd as it seemed, Mrs. Travis made her living cleaning other people's houses. I could only suppose that the people she worked for never saw her own apartment.

"Still," Susannah said, "I'd like to see it for myself. It's our only hope of finding a clue."

Few people doubt that Susannah usually knows what she's doing. Her grandmother says she takes after her grandfather, the judge, that way. So after one questioning look at Susannah, Mrs. Travis took the keys and walked us through the hedge to the Blue House.

As we crossed the creaking porch, I wasn't eager to go in. There was something forbidding about the strange old house. The shaded windows were like the eyes of a sleeping thing we'd do better not to disturb. Susannah says I have too much imagination, but just then I had a creepy feeling the house held a secret it didn't want us to know.

Inside, the place looked like a blue junk shop. I always expect things to look inside like they do on the outside, and I'm surprised when a present isn't the same color as its wrapping. The Blue House didn't disappoint me. The walls of the living room were the same faded blue as the outside, and most of the furniture was painted a brighter shade. The rest was covered in cheap fabric or Con-Tact paper, but looked just as bad. Mr. Withers hadn't done nearly as well as Pop at making junk furniture look good. In fact, he couldn't have done worse if he'd tried.

Susannah, after examining the tops of tables and looking through drawers (for letters, addresses, phone numbers or an appointment book, as I guessed), led us down the hall into the dining room. It was empty except for an ugly buffet painted blue.

"No table," Susannah remarked. "I suppose he eats in the kitchen?"

"The library." Juliet pointed across the hall. "It's his favorite room."

The library was small and coated with shelves of books. A long, gawky, homemade table filled most of the room. After glancing around, Susannah went on to the kitchen and the pantry beyond.

She pointed to a door. "That leads to the basement, I suppose. You two stay here. We'll go down." She said that to Mrs. Travis and Juliet, though personally I hadn't the least desire to explore a dark cellar.

"Look," I said, gritting my teeth so they wouldn't chatter as we went down the dimly lit stairs, "this may come as a surprise to you, but I really don't want to find a body down here."

"Me either." Susannah flicked on the light and investigated the shadowy corners. "Nothing here. Relax."

Next we all went up to the second floor. Five of the

bedrooms were empty and one was a kind of junk room—if, in this house full of junk, you could call any one room a junk room. Susannah peered inside briefly and closed the door again.

Next to the junk room was the stairway to the attic. Susannah stopped there, and for one queasy moment I was afraid I'd have to go up there with her. But after examining the steps and handrail closely, she turned away.

"Coated in dust," she commented. "He couldn't have gone up there yesterday without leaving prints on the stairs or the rail."

Only Mr. Withers' bedroom was left, a high-ceilinged room with a large bed, its tall headboard covered in blue Con-Tact paper like so much of the furniture. Mr. Withers, I reflected, must have found a good buy on blue Con-Tact paper. A quick look assured us there was nobody—and more important, no body—there. After poking in the closet, Susannah sighed with relief.

"Good," she said. "So much for the worst possibility. Mr. Withers isn't here. Now let's start figuring out where he *is*. Lucy, check the bureau and the bedside table for any slip of paper with a phone number, an address or—"

"I know," I said, opening drawers. "I don't see anything. Here's a stack of letters, but they look old."

"That's strange." Susannah was still peering into the closet. "Look at this."

It was Mr. Withers' shabby overcoat.

"Oh," said Mrs. Travis, "that's right, he was wearing his good coat—the one Ivy gave him—when he left yesterday. Funny, I never saw him wear it except to Ivy's for Christmas."

Susannah explored the pockets and pulled out a worn leather card-holder. "Medicare card, library card—he forgot all his identification. Now we're getting somewhere."

"Never mind us—where has *he* gotten, Sherlock?" I asked crisply.

"Well, I can tell you where he didn't go. He didn't go fishing, for example," Susannah said. "Not in his best clothes. In fact, it's obvious he had an important appointment somewhere out of town. Someplace rain was expected."

Mrs. Travis' eyebrows rose. "Out of town? How do you know?"

"The umbrella!" I snapped my fingers. "Of course. There wasn't a chance of rain here, so he must have been going someplace—" I groaned. "But that could be anywhere. New York or Mexico or Katmandu, for that matter."

"Not if he planned to be back to meet Juliet's bus at 3:50," Susannah pointed out. "And he didn't take a suitcase. No, it was somewhere he could get to and

back between 9:00 A.M. (when Mrs. Travis saw him leave) and 3:50 P.M. At most, seven hours. Now say he'd need at least two hours for his business and lunch"—she counted on her fingers—"and time to get to and from the bus or train station both ways—"

"Maybe he took a plane," I suggested.

"Grandpa is afraid of planes," Juliet said, and Susannah added, "Besides, poor people don't usually take planes for short trips."

"Anyway," Susannah went on, "figure at least an hour to and from the station at both ends of the trip, and that leaves less than four hours for travel time. In other words," she concluded, "wherever he went was less than two hours away by bus or train. Probably less, since he can't hurry like younger people."

I thought. "Then all we have to do is figure out where he could get to in, say, an hour and a half."

"That's one way," Susannah agreed. "Or we could find out where rain was forecast within a hundred miles or so yesterday. But I think the quickest way is to learn what buses and trains left here between about 9:30 and 10:30, then compare them with those that arrived here after 2:00 but before 3:15."

"I don't understand." Juliet gazed at us, rubbing her scar.

Susannah explained. "Your mother saw Mr. Withers leave the house about 9:00, so he couldn't have caught a bus or train much before 9:30. And probably not later than 10:30."

"And he had to get back by at least 3:30 to meet your bus at 3:50, when it stops at the corner," I continued. "But it couldn't have been earlier than 2:00, or he wouldn't have had much time for his business. So by comparing the buses and trains that left between 9:30 and 10:30 with the ones that returned between 2:00 and 3:30, we can guess where Mr. Withers went."

By now we were back in the downstairs hall by the telephone. Before I'd found the number of the train station, Susannah noticed a torn envelope stuck in the phone book. I dialed the number scrawled on it, and the bus station answered. I handed her the phone.

"We'd like to know," she stated, very businesslike, "what buses left yesterday between 9:30 and 10:30. Also what buses arrived between—" Her face went an inky purple. "Yes, my mother does know I'm phoning, and you can talk to her if you insist." She thrust the receiver at Mrs. Travis and stalked off puffing her mouth.

Mrs. Travis explained that we were hunting someone who'd caught a bus between nine-thirty and ten-thirty or so yesterday, adding pointedly that the police were searching, too. There was a pause, then she signaled Susannah to get pencil and paper.

"Monterey, San Diego, Phoenix, Sacramento, Los Angeles, New York?" Mrs. Travis repeated as Susannah scribbled. "Thank you. Now what buses arrived here between 2:00 and 3:30?"

Only two matched: the 3:20 from New York three thousand miles away, and the 2:55 from Sacramento, about eighty miles away. I grinned triumphantly at Susannah, who tried to look modest.

"We can leave the rest to the police," she said. "They'll check the Sacramento hospitals and morgue."

Then we noticed Juliet. She'd been standing all this time at her mother's elbow, her face damply white except for the burn scar. Exchanging a guilty look, Susannah and I went to comfort her.

"Hush!" Mrs. Travis tapped her foot and repeated into the phone: "What? The Sacramento bus was late? Because a man took ill—a heart attack? But please, where did they take him? . . . Yes, of course, I'll wait." Wide-eyed, she reported to us that the 2:55 bus from Sacramento had detoured at Davis for an ambulance to take a man off.

"But why didn't they try to reach us?" she wondered.

"They didn't know who he was, that's why," Susannah said. "He left all his identification in his old coat upstairs."

And he must have been too sick to tell them, I thought.

20

The voice on the phone didn't know where the sick passenger had been taken, so Mrs. Travis began dialing all the hospitals in Davis. While people on the other end of the line checked their records, Susannah and I patted Juliet's shoulder like a couple of tail-wagging dogs that longed to help but didn't know how.

Mrs. Travis' voice speaking into the phone was almost a relief. "Yes, he wore a new blue coat. That's right, a silver-handled cane. Please just tell me—is he—?" A long pause, then: "Oh, I see."

She hung up slowly. She didn't have to tell us the rest.

Three

THE DAY AFTER Mr. Withers' funeral Susannah said something awful.

"Well, it was fun while it lasted, but that's the end of the excitement for awhile."

I stared at her, horrified. "Susannah! You don't mean Mr. Withers' death was exciting. You wouldn't want—"

Susannah gave me a disgusted look over her glasses. "Of course not. In fact, his death ruined everything. There were some curious points I wanted to—" She sighed. "Well, it doesn't matter anymore."

"What points?"

Susannah cocked her head as if tackling a math problem. "Well, like why did he go to Sacramento? It must have been important since he never wore his best coat. And another thing: Who is Joe?"

"It's funny Joe didn't come to the funeral," I mused. "You suppose he didn't know? Mrs. Travis said nobody came but some neighbors and Ivy Withers and Mr. Withers' lawyer, what's-his-name?"

"Mr. Philips," said Susannah. "I think I've met him." That didn't surprise me, Susannah's grandfather being a judge. "And don't forget Miss Valentine. She was there."

"You mean that strange lady Mrs. Travis talked about—the one in the turban and the purple cape? I wonder why she came."

"Mrs. Travis says Miss Valentine and Mr. Withers were old friends. Miss Valentine owns an antique shop, you know," Susannah said. "Juliet says Mr. Withers used to buy things from her when he was rich. Then later when he needed money, he sold things to her. Nice of Miss Valentine to come to his funeral."

"Unless she was just trying to get in good with his rich niece," I pointed out. "Anyway, we can forget about Joe and the rest of it, because that's it for our first case."

But there was one point I couldn't stop thinking about. I kept wishing Mr. Withers had something to leave to Juliet. Just enough maybe to cover the operation on her cheek, which Mrs. Travis couldn't pay for.

It wasn't that the burn scar looked all that bad. When you got to know Juliet, you didn't notice it any more than Susannah's glasses or my crooked front tooth. But it made her *feel* ugly. That's why she turned her head when anybody talked to her.

"Wouldn't it be nice," I said to Juliet on the bus going home—lately we'd been sharing a seat with her and sometimes stopping off at her apartment—"Wouldn't it be nice if Mr. Withers turned out to be a rich miser who's left you his fortune?"

Susannah's nudge reminded me: We'd promised Mrs. Travis to keep Juliet from brooding about Mr. Withers.

But Juliet looked almost amused. "Grandpa a miser? Forget it. As soon as he got any money (he got a little, not much, from some insurance or something) he'd take me to the movies and buy me sodas and stuff. Then he'd have to borrow eggs and sugar from Mom till his next check came."

"Insurance?" I began eagerly, but Susannah squelched that hope. It was the kind of insurance that stopped paying when the person died, she said. She'd already checked, of course.

"Didn't Mr. Withers have *anything* valuable he could leave you?" I insisted.

Juliet sighed. "I told you: All his nice things were stolen years ago. The only thing the burglars missed was a beautiful old clock, and he finally had to sell that to Miss Valentine to pay some bills." Her lip quivered. "Poor Grandpa. He loved his antiques."

24

I wouldn't give up. "Okay, so he didn't have any money or valuable stuff. But what about his house?"

"He left it to Ivy. Mr. Philips, his lawyer, read the will yesterday. But I already knew because Grandpa told me a long time ago." Juliet turned on me as if I'd accused Mr. Withers of being unfair. "He had to leave the house to Ivy. She paid the taxes on it. He promised her."

"Oh." I didn't know what else to say.

Susannah looked at Juliet curiously. "You mean he *told* you he couldn't leave you anything? Nothing at all?"

"Well, I did think maybe . . . he said a couple of times. . . ." Juliet twisted her fingers, then faced us defiantly. "Don't you understand? Grandpa wanted to help us so much. It's just that . . . well, I think he used to forget he wasn't rich anymore."

I sat up. "Then he *did* promise you something! What?"

"Nothing. It's not important." Juliet shrugged. "Please, let's quit talking about it." She looked so miserable that, glancing at Susannah, I decided to drop it.

But when Juliet got off the bus, Susannah rubbed her glasses along her nose and muttered: "Interesting. Mr. Withers promised to leave Juliet something in his will, then didn't. Wonder why?"

"Bet he forgot he'd already sold it," I said. "If he

tried to leave Juliet something he didn't have any-more, his lawyer would have stopped him."

"You're right," said Susannah. "So let's ask his law-yer, Mr. Philips, if that's what happened. It'll make Juliet feel better to know Mr. Withers at least tried to keep his promise."

"So we go tromping up to Mr. Philips' office and demand to know exactly what was in Mr. Withers' will," I snorted. "And what makes you think a big lawyer's going to give two kids the time of day?"

"I think he will." Susannah smiled. "Especially if those kids are serving him punch and cake."

Four

AND THAT WAS HOW I came to be passing a tray of bitsy sandwiches at a reception Susannah's grandparents, Judge and Mrs. Higgins, gave for some visiting senator Saturday afternoon. Mrs. Higgins decided I'd be safer with sandwiches than punch, after I'd tripped twice on the long dress Susannah had lent me.

But we couldn't manage to corner Mr. Philips. He was always talking to the judge or the senator or Ivy Withers. Even Miss Withers got left out of his conversation at last. Looking around, she spotted Susannah.

"Ooh—" She was the kind that oohs a lot and wears a smile that even Knievel Jones wouldn't expect the teacher to believe when he's swearing he didn't trip me. "You must be the Higginses' granddaughter, the nice child who helped Mrs. Travis find my poor uncle. She said you were such a help."

"Susannah sure was," I said. "She was the one who found him, in fact. But Mrs. Travis was *such* a help."

Miss Withers looked confused. "Oh, I believe Mrs. Travis did say that." She obviously couldn't believe it. "My, aren't you a smart little girl! You'd make a good detective."

"Yes, ma'am," Susannah said. "I think I will."

"Oh, you want to become a detective? How nice. I remember at your age I wanted to be a ballerina."

The thought of prim, plump Ivy Withers cavorting about in a tutu made me jiggle the plate so that she missed her first try for a sandwich.

"I'm sorry about your uncle," Susannah said. "If you'd been home that day, maybe you could have told us where he'd gone."

"Oh no, dear. I don't know yet why he went to Sacramento. He hadn't been there in years, I'm sure."

"Maybe he went to see a friend," Susannah suggested.

Ivy Withers shook her head. "He had no friends left. So sad, too, because he used to have so many, years ago, before he lost his fortune. It was his own fault. He closed his door to everyone and became a recluse. Pride, I suppose. Only Miss Valentine, of his old friends, put up with that kind of treatment."

She gestured toward a woman in a feather boa and heavy green eyeshadow, faintly suggestive of a green-masked raccoon, who had the judge cornered.

"But except for Miss Valentine, he didn't see any-one. And of course, his cleaning woman, Mrs. Travis. Such a nice person for a cleaning woman. I mean—" She suddenly remembered that we knew Mrs. Travis.

Susannah said, "Don't forget his friend Joe—oh, what's his name?"

Ivy Withers looked blank. "Joe? Uncle never mentioned any Joe. Of course, Uncle was never very talkative with me, even when I got him to let me in." Her laugh was brittle. "I *tried* to look after him, but I'm sure everyone blames me that he looked like a tramp. I wanted to buy him some decent clothes, but he wouldn't let me."

"Maybe he liked his old clothes," I said.

"That's what he said. He could be very stubborn when he'd made up his mind to something."

"I suppose he was the same way about his furniture," Susannah remarked.

Ivy Withers made a face. "That awful junk! I offered him my perfectly good things when I bought new furniture, but he refused. Said if he couldn't have antiques, he wouldn't settle for second best."

"Nobody can accuse you of not trying to help him, Ivy," said a deep voice behind me. Mr. Philips, the lawyer, joined us. "You paid the taxes to save his house after he'd lost everything else investing in a worthless gold mine. Too bad," he added grimly, "he didn't know as much about gold mines as he did antiques."

"Antiques!" Ivy snorted. "He spent half his fortune on them, and look what happened. Every blessed one stolen, and not a dime of insurance did he have. He was *so* impractical."

"I heard about that," said Susannah. "The burglars cleaned out his house, didn't they? But how did they know the antiques were there?"

"Who *didn't* know?" Mr. Philips grimaced. "The Withers Collection was pictured in magazines. The thieves waited till he was away in Europe, then came with a van and loaded it up."

"They told the neighbors they were antique dealers who'd bought his things," Ivy put in. "People believed them because they'd heard Uncle had just lost his fortune."

"Beautiful!" Susannah whistled. "A first-class job."

Ivy Withers looked horrified.

"Oh, of course, burglars are awful," Susannah added quickly. "But we detectives have to study their methods to outwit them, you know. Excuse me, please, I think Granny wants me."

Did Mrs. Higgins *ever* want us! From her point of view, we were there to pass punch and sandwiches. We reloaded our trays and wove our way through the crowd again.

31

"Hey, if you're going to question Mr. Philips, better make it fast," I muttered to Susannah. "I think he's leaving."

Across the room Mr. Philips had his coat on and kept glancing at the door, but Miss Valentine had him cornered. Judging by his face, he yearned to wrench his elbow from her grasp and leave her talking to the air. He brightened when we popped up beside him with our trays. I think he meant to palm off Miss Valentine on us while he got away.

"Hello again, girls. Miss Valentine, this is—er, Miss Valentine—"

But Miss Valentine wasn't so easily interrupted. She went on with her story while Mr. Philips impatiently stubbed out a smoking cigar.

"Miss Valentine," he insisted when she paused for breath, "this is Judge and Mrs. Higgins' granddaughter Susannah and her friend—er—"

"Lucy," I said.

I guessed it wasn't *my* name that made Miss Valentine break off her story.

"Of course! You're the clever girl who helped that cleaning woman find my poor friend, John Withers." Her eyes on Susannah, she took a sandwich from my tray without noticing who was propping it up.

"You knew Mr. Withers pretty well, didn't you?" Susannah asked. "You must have known his friend Joe, too."

"Joe? Joe who? Everybody I know gave up on him years ago when he wouldn't let us in the house. Not that I blame him, if Ivy is right about the junk he had there. He'd have been humiliated to have his old friends see how he was living." Her green-hooded eyes roved the room like a falcon searching out prey.

"He didn't let you in?" Susannah asked.

"Well no, not exactly. But he visited my shop now and then. In fact, he sold me his eighteenth century French clock a few years ago." The falcon eyes froze on a target. "Excuse me, I must have just a word with Mrs. Higgins." She darted off, the feather boa fluttering behind.

Mr. Philips winked at us and shook his head. "Well, if you young ladies will excuse me now—"

Susannah caught his sleeve. "Mr. Philips, did Mr. Withers ever talk about making another will? I mean, did he talk about leaving somebody something that— well, maybe he didn't even have?"

Mr. Philips looked less surprised than I was at the suddeness of the question. "You're thinking of your friend, the Travis girl, aren't you?"

We nodded.

"I don't blame you. I know he loved her as if she'd been his granddaughter. I was surprised that he didn't will her his watch. You can tell her Miss Withers will see that she gets it anyway."

"But didn't he ever—" Susannah began.

34

"Ask to change his will? No," Mr. Philips finished. "Try to understand. He had nothing left but his house, and he'd promised that to Ivy for paying the taxes all these years. He'd never break his promise. John Withers was a man of his word."

Mr. Philips took the last cup from Susannah's tray and raised it in a toast, as if to a ghost. A chill ran down my spine.

"In fact"—Mr. Philips turned the empty cup in his hands—"the very day before he died, John Withers called me and asked me to read his will to him. No," he anticipated Susannah's question, "he didn't ask to change it. In fact, he seemed quite pleased with it. Though frankly, I wanted to rewrite it."

"What was wrong with it?" Susannah asked.

Mr. Philips smiled. "Nothing that would bother anyone but a lawyer. He'd written that will himself years ago, you see. I just thought it should be more precise than just 'I leave my house to Ivy Withers,' that's all."

"That sounds pretty clear to me," I said.

"No doubt." Mr. Philips shrugged and set down the glass. "It doesn't matter since there are no other relatives to contest the will. Well, I must be going now." With a half-bow to us, he turned and shouldered his way to the door.

That ended our investigations, and two detectives finished the evening as maids, cleaning up with the regular maid, Mrs. Higgins, and the honorable judge himself.

"Well, so much for that," I said to Susannah as I ran down to the judge's car for the trip home, too stuffed with party tidbits for Pop's tuna casserole. "There's no second will. No mystery. No nothing. A waste of a perfectly good afternoon I could have spent playing basketball."

"On the contrary, Lucy." Susannah's dark eyes sparkled. "Now I know for sure there *is* a second will. The next problem is to find it."

Five

"YOU MEAN MR. PHILIPS was lying?"

It was the next afternoon, a Sunday, at the Y pool. I wanted to practice some dives, and Susannah agreed that exercise might "stimulate our brain cells." But it was too noisy to think with the lifeguard blowing his whistle at Knievel Jones every two minutes. Anyway, all I really was thinking about was how to pay Knievel back for ducking me.

I saw my chance, dived and located Knievel's unsuspecting toes underwater, and was back before he'd caught his breath.

"Ready to go?" I gasped, hauling myself out of the pool.

"Good idea." Without her glasses, Susannah had missed the action. "Let's go somewhere quiet where we can think."

She probably meant the library, not behind some garbage cans in the nearest alley. But I hadn't counted on Knievel's following us with two balloons he'd filled with water right under the lifeguard's nose.

Spotting him coming, I grabbed Susannah's hand and galloped her around the corner and into the alley. Slow-witted old Knievel raced past with his fat balloons.

After I'd explained why we'd better do our thinking right there for the time being, I got back to my question: "So Mr. Philips lied to us?"

"No." Susannah peered curiously at me over her specs. "What gave you that idea?"

"You did," I snapped. "If Mr. Philips wasn't lying, what makes you so sure Mr. Withers wrote another will?"

"Because Mr. Philips and Ivy both practically told us he did. Though they don't know it themselves, of course. Come on, Lucy, *think*," she added sharply. "You heard them say that Mr. Withers never broke a promise. Remember? Ivy said he was very stubborn when he made up his mind."

I saw her point. "Yeah. If they're right, he wasn't the kind of person to make a promise to Juliet and break it." I thought that over. "But if he made another will, why didn't Mr. Philips know about it?"

"You don't need a lawyer to write a will, Lucy. Just two witnesses. A lawyer only puts it in proper legal form. Remember, Mr. Withers wrote the first will himself anyway."

I wanted to buy her idea, but something bothered me. "Everybody says Mr. Withers didn't have anything but the house. You think that's what he left to Juliet in this second will?"

Susannah shook her head. "Not if he never broke promises—and that's the reason I think there *is* a second will. No, he'd keep his promise to Ivy, too."

"Then what did he leave Juliet?"

"Something nobody knows he had—unless this mysterious Joe does. We'll know when we find the missing will, which is our next job. Correction." Susannah glanced over my shoulder. "Our next job is to get rid of your sweetheart."

"Sweetheart?" Scrambling to look over the trash can, I saw Knievel Jones leering into our alley and cuddling a plump, water-filled balloon. I had to credit him with more brains than I'd thought, to backtrack and smoke us out.

As I snatched up the lid of the trash can for a shield, I spotted a lusciously rotten apple underneath. I let Knievel have it just as he flung his bloated balloon. We both ducked, but not Susannah. *Splosh!* She got the balloon. And *splat!* my apple hit a man who had the bad luck to be passing by the entrance.

I'd rather not recall the rest of this scene. Susannah did most of the talking. Or rather, she let the man

talk while she apologized. She didn't even try to put the blame where it belonged—on Knievel Jones, who was long gone by now, of course.

So there I was, flat broke after giving the man my life savings to pay his cleaning bill.

"I'm going to get that Knievel," I swore.

While I thought how to get Knievel, Susannah was thinking how to get into the Blue House.

"We've got to find that second will before Ivy Withers sells the house."

We decided just to ask Mrs. Travis for the key. But when we went around to the apartment, she was out.

"Anyway, Mom gave the key back to Ivy Withers," said Juliet. "Why do you need it?"

"I left my sweater in the house," I lied. We'd agreed not to tell the Travises about our idea. If we were wrong, they'd get their hopes up for nothing.

"You'll have to wait till Ivy Withers comes back from vacation," Juliet said. "I'd like to get in myself. Just to kind of look around. In case Grandpa, well, did leave me some little—oh, I know I'm just wish-thinking, like Mom says. But you got me to thinking the other day."

"Thinking what?" Susannah demanded.

Juliet turned her cheek away shyly. "Well, about what Grandpa said that morning—the last time I saw

41

him. When he walked me to the bus stop." Her mouth twitched and she looked away.

"Go on," I urged. "What did he say?"

Juliet hesitated. "Oh, nothing—just something about some 'treasure,' he called it. He acted really excited and kept saying, 'Now you can have my treasure someday.'"

"What treasure?" I demanded.

"Oh, I'm sure it's only some little thing—"

"What else did he say?" Susannah interrupted. "Think now, Juliet. Tell me his exact words."

Juliet looked embarrassed. "Just something about a 'good man.' It didn't make any sense. Something about this 'good man' helping with the treasure. In fact, his last words as I got on the bus were: 'Remember, Juliet, see a good man.' Oh, I wish I'd listened better, but how was I to know?"

"'See a good man,'" Susannah mused. "And then he left for Sacramento. Maybe he meant the man he went to see."

"Oh great," I snorted. "So now we know there's one good man in Sacramento. That's nice. But our problem right now, if you'll excuse me for reminding you two, is: How do we get into the Blue House?"

Juliet said slowly, "Grandpa used to keep a spare key hidden somewhere. I don't know where exactly. But even if we find it, I don't think we ought to go in the house without permission."

"Me either," Susannah admitted, "however—"

I lost all patience. "Look, are you two going to wait around until Ivy comes back? If she finds the will before we do, forget it."

Juliet looked shocked. "Miss Withers wouldn't keep anything that Grandpa left me."

"Oh yeah?" I scoffed.

Susannah opened the back door. "I'm more afraid that Ivy Withers might throw it out by accident. A will is just a piece of paper. Anyway, there's no harm in looking for an old key, is there?"

Juliet and I couldn't see any.

I've never gotten to know a yard, front and back, as I did Mr. Withers' yard. We started with the obvious places: in the mailbox, over the doorframe, under the doormat. We must have looked under ten dozen flowerpots. We peered beneath doorsteps and on window ledges and in the birdbath. We even lifted the loose head of a moss-covered statue. Then we paced the yard, looking for any kind of hiding place.

"Didn't Mr. Withers ever hint where he hid the key?" Susannah mopped her forehead.

"No," said Juliet. "He always said a little bird gave it to him."

Not even funny, I thought, clambering up the fence to scan the crossrail. I didn't see a key there, but I did see a mop of red hair on the other side.

I don't know how long Knievel Jones had been spying on us through the broken slat. I only know I resisted the urge to let him have it with the ripe persimmon on the branch by my elbow, since I didn't want him chasing me into the yard just now. So I politely asked what his ugly carcass was doing there. He, equally polite, wanted to know what us "bat brains" were up to, prowling around Mr. Withers' yard.

"It's an Easter egg hunt," I said, eyeing the persimmon wistfully.

"In October?" Now he was really suspicious.

I had to get rid of him before he climbed the fence. I thought fast. "If you must know, we're planning a séance."

"A what?"

"Séance. You know, where you contact ghosts. We're going to get in touch with Mr. Withers' spirit."

Knievel looked incredulous. "Go on. You don't believe in ghosts."

"Huh. What do you know about it?" I tried to sound mysterious. "Lots of people talk to ghosts in séances."

"Whew," Knievel whistled. "You're even dumber than I thought. Let me get out of here." Hooting with laughter, he started off on the battered bicycle he pretends is a real Harley-Davidson motorcycle.

"Yeah, you better run!" I yelled. "Before you meet one of those ghosts you don't believe in. You haven't got the guts to—"

Susannah's yelp made me forget Knievel Jones. She was looking up a tree.

"I think I know the little bird that kept Mr. Withers' key." She grinned. "At least, I bet that's his house."

I boosted her up to the birdhouse. While I grunted and sweated, she fumbled in the hole and at last drew out a key.

Juliet and I were all for going into the Blue House right then, but Susannah's watch showed that it was nearly time to be getting home.

"Let's wait till we have plenty of time," she said. "It may not be easy to find what we're looking for."

As we crossed through the hedge, Juliet said, "Let's don't tell my mom yet. I don't want to get her hopes up for nothing. Right now she's pretty worried about money."

That suited us, since we were afraid Mrs. Travis might put a stop to our plans to search the house.

"You still haven't told us, Juliet," said Susannah before we left, "what kind of treasure you think Mr. Withers left you. Didn't he say?"

"Not exactly." Juliet rubbed her burn scar thoughtfully. "He *did* say a couple of times that he wanted me to have—it doesn't sound very valuable—"

"Yes, yes," I snapped. "Just say—what was it?"

"I can't remember the name exactly," Juliet said, "but it was a book. Some kind of history book."

"A book!" I croaked, about as disappointed as you can get.

Six

As it turned out, we didn't get into the Blue House all the next week. Even with a key, it was no easy matter just to sashay through the front door in full view of the neighbors. No matter how we figured it, we couldn't think of a way to do it unnoticed. Until that Friday.

Mrs. Travis had planned a special party for Juliet's birthday. "It's going to be the best she's ever had," she said, "to make up for all her sadness this fall." It was to be a wiener roast and treasure hunt. Mrs. Travis had invited our whole class.

Susannah and I were going to spend the night together afterwards. We did that so often that our folks hardly bothered checking with each other any-more. So I arrived at the party with my gift and a paper bag stuffed with pajamas. The first person I saw was Susannah with her gift and the knapsack she always carried her pajamas in.

"Why did you bring your pajamas?" we both said at the same time. "We're sleeping at *your* house."

"Remember, we decided your house was closer," Susannah said.

"I told you Pop won't be home till late. Well, what do you want to do?"

Susannah's grin told me *exactly* what we were going to do. "It's fate," she whispered. "Our folks think we're at each other's house, and we'll never have a better chance. As soon as we can get away from here—"

Juliet rushed up, looking relieved to see us. She'd been standing against the wall staring at her guests. Thinking about our plans, I absent-mindedly handed her a package.

"Thanks a lot," she said, opening it. "Just what I wanted: pajamas and—oh wow!—a toothbrush. Looks like it's hardly been used, too."

I snatched back the paper bag and gave her the gift. But I was glad to see her grinning at last.

I hardly recognized the place. The dining table, cleared of paints and teacups and laundry, held a huge cake frosted with flowers and butterflies. The closets must have been bulging, for the apartment was a credit to Mrs. Travis' reputation among the families she cleaned for, and a smell of ammonia and wax hung on the air. It was a credit to her artistry, too, for among the purple and orange streamers hung paper sculptures of Alice in Wonderland's Cheshire cat, the Caterpillar, Mad Hatter and the rest.

When everybody had arrived and the table was heaped with gifts, we went outside. Mrs. Travis had borrowed a barbecue and had hot dogs and buns ready. Funny how much better frankfurters taste blistered on one side and raw on the other than they do cooked on a stove.

It was getting dark by now. I couldn't help glancing uneasily at the gloomy old house next door and wondering if I really wanted to explore it tonight.

"Maybe we ought to wait till tomorrow," I mumbled. "It'll be easier to see things in the daylight. Besides, Juliet can't leave her party, and we can't just desert her. We're her only friends here."

"It has to be tonight," Susannah insisted. "It's our only chance. Anyway, I think Juliet's made a new friend." That was true, for Juliet was busy talking to another girl on the other side of the barbecue. "Don't worry about getting around in the dark," she added. "I brought my flashlight."

"That's nice. . . ." Then the awful truth hit me. "You mean there're no lights in the house? *We're going to be in the dark?*"

"The electricity's probably still on," said Susannah, "but we can't risk turning on lights. Somebody's bound to see."

While I wondered whether Susannah would believe me if I suddenly developed appendicitis, the treasure hunt began. We took partners and chose a clue from the bowl of folded papers. Juliet teamed up with her new friend, and Susannah and I claimed each other as partners.

"Now's our chance to slip over to the Withers' house," Susannah whispered. "We'll tell Mrs. Travis and Juliet we have to leave because you're sick." Which, in fact, wasn't far from the truth.

Luckily, Mrs. Travis was too busy to ask questions when we made our excuse. Juliet, exploring the garage with her partner, looked disappointed but said she hoped I'd feel better, and went back to hunting their hidden clue. So now we were free to go.

But when we reached the opening in the hedge, we met two girls who had just figured out that their clue—"Prickly to touch and sweet to taste; you'll find a clue there if your time you don't waste"—meant the blackberries there. So we wandered off to wait by the garbage cans. And there, you might know, we found Knievel Jones.

"Aw, your folks lock you out again?" I said sympathetically. "Here, I'll let you in." I lifted the garbage can lid and sidestepped his punch.

"Excuse me," he sneered, "didn't know this was yours. Thought you still lived at the city dump. What happened, your dad finally decide to get a job so you could live better?"

I was about to show Knievel what a lousy sense of humor he had, but Susannah grabbed my arms.

"Stop it!" she hissed in my ear. "You want to ruin Juliet's party and get sent home besides? Cool down and help me get rid of him." Out loud she said, "You're too late, Knievel. We finished the hot dogs and cake."

"Me go to a dumb party?" Kneivel gave a good imitation of being sick. "Just wondered what was causing all the yelling and running around, that's all. I live back there." He jerked his thumb at the building behind Juliet's.

Clearly he wasn't going to leave till he found out, so we told him about the treasure hunt. Of course, he thought it was the dumbest thing he'd ever heard of. But he couldn't resist snatching our clue.

"'Sitting on this you go to and fro. Maybe you'd rather look for a clue there, though,'" he read.

"Now what can that mean?" Susannah frowned. "I can't figure it out."

"Huh." Knievel scratched his head. "'Go to and fro'—that's backwards and forwards. Hey, I bet it's a swing."

"Of course!" Susannah snapped her fingers. "I never would have thought of it. There are swings in the park around the corner, and some behind the church. Wonder which it means?"

"It means—YEEK!" I yelped as she poked my ribs, and I realized that she was up to something. Which certainly relieved my mind, for I was wondering why the great detective couldn't see Juliet's rope swing on the tree not ten feet away. "I mean, we better check both places."

"Tell you what," said Susannah. "Since you figured out the clue, Knievel, we'll let you join us. We're sure to win the prize, and I hear it's a big one."

"A big prize?" Knievel's greedy eyes widened. "Okay, you're on. You check the church swings while I run up to the park." And he was off.

A moment later we were off, too. Susannah hustled me through the hedge and into the shadowy, over-grown yard next door. Looking up at the vast, dark old house, I wished I'd gone looking for the swings.

Seven

THE HOUSE SEEMED to watch from behind shaded windows as we came. Looking up at the grim, ruined towers, I had a panicky feeling that they would come crashing down on us.

Susannah turned the key and the door screeched open. I jumped.

"Remember now, we can't turn on any lights." Susannah's matter-of-fact voice steadied me. She pulled me inside, shut the door and fumbled with the flashlight. "Darn this switch, it keeps sticking. Hold on, I'll get it working in a minute."

It was chilly inside and deathly still. The air smelled musty. At first I could see nothing. Then as my eyes adjusted to the dim streetlight through the shades, I saw that the purplish darkness was lumpy with mysterious shapes. For a moment they seemed to me the ghosts of Mr. Withers' long-vanished antiques. I blinked and saw the room in its days of glory, filled with priceless satin chairs, polished tables and velvet sofas from long ago.

Then Susannah flicked on the flashlight, and the vision vanished. The ghostly shapes became what they really were: worthless junk painted blue or covered in scraps of plastic and cheap fabric. I shook myself.

"Nothing here," Susannah muttered, slamming drawers and opening cabinets, most of which contained little but old magazines. "Lucy, are you just going to stand there all night?"

Zipping up my jacket (for I was suddenly cold), I forced myself to open the nearest drawer. Between us we checked every place we could think of in ten minutes.

"I don't see anyplace else here that he was likely to put a will." Susannah flashed the light around the room. "It's probably either in his bedroom or the library, which Juliet says was his favorite room."

"Let's try the library," I said quickly, being none too eager to climb those dark stairs. I followed her down the gloomy hall, sticking close behind the comforting light. Inside the library Susannah closed the door and turned on the small table lamp. It was safe to do because the one narrow window faced a wall of the kitchen.

We blinked at the sudden brightness and looked around. Three sides of the small room were covered with books—hundreds and hundreds of books, more than I could imagine anyone ever reading. The large, ugly table took up most of the remaining space. Of all the grotesque furniture in the house, this was probably the worst because it was so big. The top was sheathed in imitation-wood Con-Tact paper, and the legs seemed to be four upended crates.

"Look at that." I nodded at the table. "For a man who was supposed to know so much about furniture, he didn't know the first thing about making his own. I could do lots better." I could, too. I'd have bought a door from a lumberyard, like Pop did for our dining table, and screwed on those metal legs you can buy.

Susannah grunted. "Never mind the table. Just look for the will."

There wasn't a drawer or cabinet in the room. Nothing but that hideous table, two lumpy, slip-covered chairs, and lots and lots of books. I couldn't see anyplace to look.

"Books," Susannah mused. "I wonder now. Mr. Withers told Juliet about a history book. Could that be where he hid the will? But which book?"

I followed her eye up and down the endless shelves. "No," I croaked. "You crazy? We can't go through all those books tonight when we don't even know the title or—"

Susannah sighed. "You're right, it'll take ages. Maybe first we better search upstairs."

The last thing I wanted was to leave this cozily lighted room to go prowling in the darkness upstairs. "On second thought," I said quickly, "we really ought to check out this room carefully while we're here. It won't take long."

"Good thinking," Susannah agreed. "Now, notice how the books are arranged?"

"All I notice is that they're mostly older than George Washington's grandma. Wait a minute." I scanned a shelf carefully. "These are all poetry books. And the next one is—yep, all travel books."

"I thought so," said Susannah. "They're all arranged by subject, like in a real library."

We scanned the shelves excitedly, looking for the history section. There seemed to be books on everything: birds, insects, humor, philosophy, even fairy tales.

"Here's a history book!" I cried out. Then looking at it closely, my hopes fell. "No, it isn't. It's just about old castles and stuff. *Historical Mansions of Cro—Cro—*" I gave up on the word and shoved the book at Susannah.

"Cro— Croatia," she floundered through the syllables. "Where's that, I wonder? Anyway, it's not a real history book. See? This whole shelf seems to be books about antiques."

Then I saw the history books. "Susannah, look!" There were five full shelves of them from floor to ceiling. The shelf I pointed to held sixteen red leather volumes titled *A Brief History of the World*. But as Susannah believes in being systematic, we dragged up chairs and started with the top shelf.

I never knew there was so much history. Or so many places I'd never heard of—Byzantium and Serbia and Belize and Zanzibar and good old Croatia again. I examined the books every which way I could think of, looking down the spines, flipping pages, feeling the endsheets for anything hidden under them. I got so interested I almost forgot we were alone in a dark, creepy house. Until I heard a sound upstairs.

Susannah heard it, too. We stood like stones, holding our breath and listening.

Susannah let out her breath and grinned. "Just a door banging shut in a draft. The wind's come up—hear?"

We finished the books on the upper shelves and were down to the sixteen red volumes of *A Brief History of the World*. Then it happened.

I reached for Volume One and Susannah tugged at Volume Sixteen at the other end. The books looked tightly wedged, so we gave a hard yank. And with a succulent ripping sound, the backs of all sixteen volumes came away in our hands, all in one long piece of red leather. Only there weren't any books behind it. Just a smooth expanse of wood with hand holds.

"A secret drawer!" I whispered.

Susannah said nothing, but opened the drawer.

Inside everything was arranged neatly: a clump of receipts clipped together, a stack of letters in a rubber band, a box of stationery, some pens and pencils, and two fat brown envelopes labeled Clippings and Important Documents. Susannah emptied the second envelope on the table and moved the lamp closer.

"Let's see. Old driver's license, warranty on a water heater . . ." Susannah shuffled through papers and laid them aside. "Tax receipts . . . What's this? Oh, his passport. Must be the one he used for that trip to Europe, the time all his antiques were stolen."

I'd never seen a passport before. "Wow, look at all those places he went—England, France, Italia (must mean Italy), Greece, Jugo— Jugo— huh? What's that?"

"Yugoslavia probably." Susannah tucked the passport and the other papers back into the envelope.

"Where's that?"

"In Europe. Come on, this isn't a geography lesson. We're looking for a will, remember?"

Too bad we *didn't* pay more attention to geography just then. There were some things that even Susannah didn't know.

Next we emptied the envelope marked Clippings, which held articles and pictures cut from magazines

and newspapers, mainly about antiques Mr. Withers had once owned. It was strange looking at pictures taken in this very house long years ago. There was one of the library itself I could hardly believe: A dainty gold-leaf desk and bowlegged chairs with satin seats perched on a beautiful rug. Looking around at the clumsy huge table and lumpy chairs now on the faded beige carpet, I could see why Mr. Withers had gone a bit crazy.

"Hey, look at this." Another clipping caught my eye. "It's all about the robbery. Wow, those burglars really wiped him out."

Susannah bent over me and followed my finger along the yellowed lines of print. ". . . Tried to contact the owner, John B. Withers, but our reporter learned that he is on a train back to California after landing in New York from Europe two days ago. Meanwhile the police say they have no clues. . . ." Susannah sighed and slipped the clipping back into the envelope. "What a rotten homecoming, and especially after he'd just learned that he was flat broke. Mr. Philips called him just after his ship landed in New York, to tell him he'd lost all his money on that phony gold mine."

We put the Clippings envelope back into the secret drawer and took out the packet of letters, which Susannah divided between us.

"Look for anything from Sacramento," she reminded

me. "Even if we don't find the will here, there must be something to tell us who his friend Joe is, or the 'good man' he went to see that last day."

But all the letters I read through seemed to be nothing more than short notices that some company or other was shipping something Mr. Withers had bought years ago, and none came from Sacramento or was signed by anyone named Joseph or Josiah or anything remotely like Joe.

"Strange," muttered Susannah as we tucked the letters back under the rubber band, then into the secret drawer. "There *must* be something here."

Just then the little lamp on the table dimmed and slowly went out. Everything vanished into darkness.

Susannah muttered, clicking the switch to her flashlight. A moment later its welcome beam shot across the room. "I remember seeing some light bulbs in the kitchen," she said. "Wait here while I go get one."

I didn't like being left alone in the dark, but I wasn't about to admit it. So I sat there cool as you please, waiting for her to come back and trying to think about other things. Like what was happening at Juliet's party, and how I was going to fix Knievel Jones, and whether Pop would buy me some boots I wanted.

And just then the ceiling squeaked. Not once, but twice—three times—four—I counted. Like someone crossing the floor above.

Eight

THE BURST OF LIGHT in the doorway blinded me. I stumbled forward, aiming a heavy dictionary.

"What on earth's the matter with you?" demanded Susannah behind the light.

I dropped the dictionary, my knees still quivering. "I—I heard a noise. Like someone walking upstairs—*listen!*" There were two sharp squeaks on the ceiling.

Susannah cocked an ear. "You goon, it's just the floorboards contracting. Old houses always squeak at night when it gets cold."

"Yeah? Well, how come *these* squeaks walked right down the hall?" I traced the path in the air with my finger.

Susannah grinned and shook her head. "Lucy! Don't tell me you of all people are going scaredy on me."

"Who me?" I tried to sound scornful, but my chattering teeth ruined it. "But maybe we ought to be going. It's getting late."

"There's still time." Susannah glanced at her watch. "And I want to do two things before we leave."

"Okay then." I tried to look as if it didn't matter to me. "Only don't blame me if we get arrested for burglary." But it wasn't fear of the police that made me lock the door and drag a chair in front of it. Susannah might be right about the floorboards, but I wasn't betting my life on it.

"First," said Susannah when the lamp was on again, "start taking down those history books again. Read me the titles and authors and the dates they were published."

"Huh?"

"It's an idea I got out in the kitchen, thinking about what you said—about the books being so old. My grandfather just paid a hundred-and-fifty dollars for an old book."

"A hundred-and-fifty dollars!"

"That's nothing. Granddaddy says some old books sell for thousands. Hey, get moving." Susannah took a pencil and a sheet of paper from the secret drawer. "We haven't got all night."

Half an hour later we had a list of twenty-three history books, after Susannah had rejected those she'd seen somewhere else. Just to be sure, we added a couple of others that had something about history in the title, like *History of Italian Furniture* and *Historical Mansions of Croatia*.

"Will your grandfather know how much they're worth?" I put the last one back.

"I don't think so." Susannah zipped the list into her purse. "But he'll know somebody to ask—"

"Sh!" I stiffened.

Susannah listened. "That's just a branch brushing the kitchen window. I noticed it while I was out there. Really, Lucy, you're beginning to make *me* jumpy."

"Jumpy?—I'm not jumpy." And just then a floorboard in the corner squeaked and I nearly leaped out of my socks.

Susannah didn't seem to notice. "Well, I think we're finished here." She turned off the lamp and flicked on her flashlight, which promptly went out again. "Darn that switch. Ah, there," as it went back on. "Now for upstairs."

The sigh of relief strangled in my throat. "Upstairs?"

"Of course, upstairs. Lucy, this may be our only chance to find the will."

"But you said the books might be worth a lot of money."

"We don't know for sure." Susannah's voice was patient. "Anyway they don't belong to Juliet unless we find that second will."

I sighed miserably. "Susannah, I still think I heard something up there."

"Look," said Susannah, "if you'd rather wait down here—come to think of it, you could be searching the buffet in the dining room. I saw a candle and matches in the kitchen."

Somehow the idea of being alone in the dining room with a candle didn't appeal to me either.

"I can't let you go upstairs by yourself," I said.

Susannah hugged me. "You're a real friend."

So together we followed the flashlight down the hall and up the creaking stairs. They creaked so loudly that maybe, I hoped, whatever might be upstairs would be scared away. Maybe.

At the top, Susannah sprayed the flashlight along the hall, brushing the double row of doors and the stairway to the attic. The hall was empty and still.

Somehow we didn't dare break the silence. We scuttered into the bedroom and closed the door.

If the high-ceilinged bedroom had been gloomy in the daylight, it was downright eerie by flashlight. The narrow beam of light picked out bare floors, tall curtained windows, the huge grotesque bed, a large bureau, a nightstand and two chairs. Even so, the huge room seemed half empty after the junk-stuffed downstairs.

"Now I wonder where—?" Something moved and Susannah jerked the flashlight toward the window.

It was only the heavy curtain stirring in a breeze. The window was ajar.

"Careless of Mrs. Travis to leave a window open," Susannah muttered. I suspected I wasn't the only one who'd just had a scare. "Well, let's get to work. You start with the bureau while I check the nightstand."

"We can't do both at the same time with only one flashlight," I pointed out, not knowing why I whispered.

"Darn, that's right." Susannah snapped her fingers. I noticed that she whispered, too. "I should have brought that candle I found. I'll have to go get it."

"I'll go with you," I said quickly.

"Okay. No, wait. Time's running short, so why don't you stay here and search? Here, take the flashlight. I can find my way down in the dark."

"But—"

"I don't mind, honest," she said. "You know what to look for. I'll be right back. Or maybe while I'm down, I'll give that buffet a good going over first."

"But—"

The door closed behind her. I had a wild urge to race out behind her. Instead, I took a deep breath, told myself there was nothing to be afraid of, and shoved a chair against the door.

"Now," I said aloud, trying to drown out the squeaks as Susannah went downstairs, "first the bureau."

I began pawing through the top drawer. Under the socks and handkerchiefs I found a few old bills and a notepad. I took a few minutes to decipher the scribbles on the pad (which wasn't easy with the flashlight dancing in my jittery hand), but they turned out to be reminders like *Buy birdseed* and *Water morning glories.* The other drawers contained only shirts, pajamas and underwear. I shoved the drawers back. They wouldn't close all the way, but I was in no mood to be fussy.

"So much for that." It was comforting to hear even my own voice in the black silence. "Now for the nightstand." I swept the light over the room. Then I froze.

Out of the darkness a hideous demon face leered at me.

I must have a strong heart. Anyway, I didn't drop dead or faint or even scream. Actually, I did start to scream, but before I got my breath, I knew that the demon was only a queer lump in the headboard of the bed. A warp in the wood under the Con-Tact paper, probably. The flashlight cast shadows that gave it a nose and eyes—if you could call them eyes. Even knowing it wasn't real, I shivered.

I pulled my eyes away and forced my attention on the nightstand. It took me less than two minutes to decide there wasn't any will in the drawer. Just a stack of letters that looked pretty old, some playing cards, and a paperback book.

"What a dumb waste of time!" I grumbled to the darkness, backing toward the door. "Nothing here we didn't see the last time."

I don't know what made me flash the light over the bed just then—perhaps I wanted to see if it was still there—but suddenly the demon face sprang out of the dark again. It hung there in the little circle of light, fixing its sightless eyes on me in a sly, unsmiling, evil gaze. That was the last thing I saw before the flashlight went out.

I had flicked off the switch in my panic, and now I couldn't get it on again. My sweaty fingers tried to force it. I shook it, cursed it, tried everything I could think of. The light did not come back on.

I threw down the flashlight, shoved the chair from the door and plunged into the hall. I blundered a few feet through the darkness, then stopped in fresh horror. Don't ask me to explain how I knew: Someone was there.

Then I touched a wall and gratefully promised God to go to church next Sunday. Now if I could only find the stairs, I'd even be good—honest, I'd even be nice to Knievel Jones. I prayed as I slid my hands over doors and walls. With one hand I hunted for the staircase while the other, reaching higher, sought the light switch. It wasn't the light switch my arm connected with, but something softer and warmer. Something that went *Uff!* as I walloped it and ran.

For at that same moment my left hand found the stair rail, and gripping it, I took the stairs in leaps with only one thought in my mind: *Get out of here!* I forgot about wills, I forgot mysteries, I forgot Susannah.

The question was: Where was the front door? Panicked, I turned and slammed right into something. Something soft but solid. Something that went *Uff!* again. Something that this time passed its hands over my face and said: "Lucy! Is that you? Girl, you scared me to death!"

I was never so glad to hear Susannah's voice.

"But where's your flashlight, Lucy? Lord, you're brave to be prowling around in the dark!"

"Susannah! Oh, I'm so glad it's you! But why didn't you say something when I ran into you upstairs?"

"Upstairs?" Susannah sounded puzzled. "I wasn't upstairs. I've been in the dining room. My candle burned out and I couldn't find the matches in the dark."

I let that information sink into my brain, then not stopping to explain, I grabbed her hand and pulled her after me.

"Let's get out of here."

She didn't argue. We felt our way along the wall in silence until we came to a door. Praying that it led to the living room, I opened it. We went a few feet before my hand touched a piece of furniture.

"The buffet," whispered Susannah. "We're back in the dining room."

We retraced our steps to the hall and turned left. We hadn't gone far before Susannah pulled me to a halt, gripping my arm in urgent warning. I'd heard it, too: a soft footstep, the creak of a door and a quick indrawing of breath somewhere close. Somebody was in the hall with us.

I don't know how long we froze against the wall before I realized that the hard thing pressing my head was a light switch. I reached back and flipped it on.

Suddenly the hall was flooded with blinding light. Blinking painfully, I saw the ghastly face before us.

"Oh no!" I groaned.

Nine

KNIEVEL JONES LOOKED as scared as we were.

"Y—you!" he squeaked, dropping his fists. "I th—thought it w—was—"

"A ghost?" finished Susannah, recovering her wits.

"C—course not. There's no such th—things as g—ghosts!" But his chalky face and stammer didn't convince me.

I could almost have kissed his repulsive face. At least it wasn't as bad as what I'd expected. And the red splotch on his chin told me what I'd run into upstairs. But as my knees stopped shaking, I began to get mad.

"What are you doing here?" I demanded, my voice still trembling. "You've got a nerve breaking into this house."

"Yeah, well what about you?" Knievel blustered squeakily. "Who invited *you*?"

"We've got business—" I blurted out.

Susannah elbowed my ribs. "But how *did* you get in, Knievel?"

"Easy." Knievel smirked. "Up the tree, onto the roof, and through the window. Nothing to it."

"Lucky you didn't break your neck."

"That's lucky?" I snarled.

"But why?" Susannah demanded. "Why go to all that troubled?"

"Knievel will go to any trouble to be a pest," I said.

Knievel curled his lip at me. "I wanted to see what you two were up to that you didn't want anybody to know about. You think I'd let you send me off on a goose chase hunting swings and not do something about it?"

"But how did you know we were here?" asked Susannah.

"Lucy told me. Well, you *did*," Knievel insisted as I sputtered my innocence to a stunned Susannah. "You said you were going to contact Mr. Withers' ghost, so I figured that's what you were up to tonight."

"To bad you missed the séance," I said sweetly, "and didn't get to see the ghost. Last we saw of him, he went floating back upstairs. By the way, where did you get that bruise on your chin?"

Knievel's eyes widened. "Go on, that was one of you up there . . . wasn't it?"

Susannah and I looked innocent. "Upstairs? We

never went upstairs," I protested with great sincerity.

"You're lying." Knievel glanced uneasily at each of us. Then with elaborate unconcern, he added, "I got to be going home now."

"Me too," I said fervently, and to my relief, Susannah agreed.

Taking our bearings first, we switched out the hall light and stumbled through the dark to the front door. Funny, squeaky floorboards in the dark aren't so scary when you have company. A bit exciting, in fact. Though once or twice, I admit, I reached for their hands in the dark and even Knievel's felt comforting.

On the porch at last, we sucked in the clean autumn air, grateful to be in the real world again. Never had stars seemed so lively as they dodged in and out among the clouds, or rhododendron bushes so joyous, swaying in the night breezes.

Susannah checked that the front door had locked behind us, then dropped the key into the mailbox. We were in no mood to put it back in the birdhouse where Mr. Withers had left it.

The party was over next door at the Travises'. Luckily, we'd thought to stash our pajama rolls in the hedge, so we didn't have to go in and explain to Mrs. Travis and Juliet, who thought we'd long since gone home.

We decided to go to my house. It was closer and

Pop was likely to come home later, or anyway ask fewer questions, than Susannah's folks. He figured that as long as I was with Susannah, it must be okay. He'd never dream we'd walk eight blocks home after dark.

Knievel walked with us. After a few blocks, Susannah gave him a curious look. "Don't your mother and father wonder where you are this time of night?"

Knievel curled his lip. "My father doesn't wonder because he hasn't seen me for four years. And Mom is out tonight."

"Don't you have a baby-sitter?"

"Baby-sitter? At my age? I told Mom I won't stand for any baby-sitter."

"And I'll bet no baby-sitter can stand you, either," I said. "But doesn't somebody check up on you?"

"Naw," Knievel boasted. "Oh, the old lady next door is supposed to see that I go to bed. But after she turns out the light, there's nothing to stop me from climbing down the fire escape."

"Neat," I breathed enviously, wondering if it was really so bad to be neglected, as I'd overheard the teacher say Knievel was. "Wish I could get out that easy."

"Then how *do* you get out?"

"We don't," said Susannah.

"Oh yeah?" Knievel laughed knowingly. "Now come on, tell the truth," he added confidentially as we rounded a corner, "what were you really up to in that creepy old house?" I knew he had a reason for walking us home.

"We told you—" Susannah began.

"Don't give me that garbage," Knievel sneered. "Lucy's dumb enough to believe in ghosts—not brave enough to go hunting one, though"—he sidestepped my kick—"but not you. You can't tell me Susannah 'The Brain' Higgins would pass up a treasure hunt she could win in her sleep to go chasing ghosts."

"Okay, what then, O Sherlock?" Susannah said drily.

"No, *you're* the one that wants to be a detective," said Knievel. "Everybody knows that. I'm just guessing that a big detective like you would only pass up that treasure hunt for a bigger and better mystery."

"You're not a bad detective youself." Susannah sounded respectful. "The only trouble with your theory is that it's wrong. We told you: We had a séance, that's all."

"Yeah? Well, just try telling that to the police," Knievel snapped, "when they find out you've been prowling in that house at night."

Susannah spun around to face him. "Don't you threaten us. You can't tell anybody without admitting that you were there, too. And another thing"—she crowded him into the gutter—"I was just thinking of asking you to work with us, if we *should* find a mystery. I thought you had possibilities. But now I see you can't be trusted. Susannah Higgins doesn't deal with blackmailers."

"Blackmailer? Who you calling a blackmailer?" Knievel stumbled out of the gutter. "I won't fink on you. And not because I'm afraid of getting in trouble myself. I could honestly tell the police I only wanted to find out what's been going on all those nights."

We'd reached my building, and a pair of headlights was turning into the drive.

"Lucy!" Pop called from our car. "Why aren't you at Susannah's?"

I explained about the mistake, meantime wondering where Susannah and Knievel had got to. A minute later she came trotting up alone.

"You should have taken your key," Pop scolded. "How long have you poor kids been waiting here?"

"Doesn't matter," I mumbled. "Well, goodnight." And I nudged Susannah toward the house.

"What does he care *where* I was," I moaned, flinging myself on my bed. "Bet he's been out with that woman again."

"What woman?" asked Susannah.

"How do I know? I never met her, but he talks about her all the time. It's Mae this and Mae that, Mae everything, till I want to barf."

"So what? You know your father takes out ladies. Oh. You're afraid he's going to marry her, aren't you?"

I shot up. "Her? Marry her? You think Pop's crazy?"

Susannah listened patiently. Thank heaven she didn't give me advice or tell me things weren't so bad. She waited until, exhausted, I quit talking and crawled under the covers. Then she broke it to me: what she'd learned from Knievel.

"Know why he thought we'd been fooling around in the Blue House before tonight?"

"Why?"

"Because he can see the house from his bedroom window. And the last three nights he's seen a flashlight moving around in there."

Ten

I DIDN'T SLEEP MUCH that night. The conversation before we turned out the lights wasn't exactly like a lullaby.

"You sure it wasn't just a plain old burglar?" I insisted for the third time.

Susannah sighed. "Would a plain old burglar come back night after night, after finding nothing worth stealing the first time? No, it had to be someone who was looking for something."

"Ivy Withers," I said flatly.

"But why would she be prowling her own house with a flashlight? Why not turn on the lights? For that matter, why search at night when she could easily search in the daytime?"

"Who could it be then?"

"Lots of people. Anybody who knew Mr. Withers well enough to learn about the valuable thing he kept secret. Take for example, the two people nobody seems to know."

"Joe, you mean? And the 'good man' in Sacramento?"

"Right." Susannah's huge dark eyes brooded. "They must know something we don't. Remember, Mr. Withers went to see them both that last day."

I shivered. "You think one of them's the prowler?"

"Very likely." She squirmed under the covers. "If only we had some clue to who they are! All we know is that Joe lives somewhere close to the Blue House."

I started up. "How do we know that?"

"It's obvious," Susannah said. "Mr. Withers never left his house for long, yet he visited Joe once or twice every week. Besides, that last morning he told Mrs. Travis he meant to see Joe, and we know he had less than an hour to make his bus. So Joe must live nearby."

"Somewhere between the Blue House and the bus station," I reflected. "Is there any way of finding him?"

"We're sure going to try," Susannah said. "Tomorrow we'll walk from the Blue House to the bus station and ask all the storekeepers if they remember seeing Mr. Withers. Maybe with luck—"

"But tomorrow we've got to send that list of books to the dealer your grandfather knows."

"That too." Susannah turned out the light. "It's going to be a busy day, so get some sleep."

I tried, but as soon as I closed my eyes, I remembered something. "Susannah, I can't go with you tomorrow. Pop and I are going to buy my boots." But her breathing told me she was asleep.

I squirmed half the night before I got to sleep finally, then dreamed we found Joe, who greeted us with a machine gun and an evil smile. "Hear you've been looking for me," he wheezed through his cigarette. "Come in and meet the Good Man." I started awake and wondered awhile if it was all just a dream. Suppose Mr. Withers was mixed up with the Mafia?

I awoke again to the clamor of Pop banging a pan on the door. I shuffled to the kitchen in a rotten mood, which wasn't improved by Pop's cheerful announcement: "Gobble it up fast, girls. I'm waiting to paint the kitchen."

That was the first I'd heard of it.

"You can't, not today." I slid into the bench at the table. It was the table that reminded me of the one in Mr. Withers' library, except that Pop had done a better job. "You're buying my boots today, remember?"

Pop bit his lip. "Darn, that's right." Scowling, he shoveled scrambled eggs onto my plate. "You don't mind going alone, do you, princess? You know what you want, and my friend Mae's coming over to help me paint the kitchen." He took out his wallet and peeled off some bills. "You don't mind, do you?"

" 'Course not." I stuffed the bills in my pocket. "Ready to go, Susannah?" Leaving my eggs on my plate, I bounded out of the kitchen. "His friend!" I muttered.

Susannah joined me a few minutes later, looking as if she was still swallowing breakfast. "Hey, girl, what's eating you? How come you treat your father like your enemy?"

"What's it to you?" I shook off her arm and started down the street.

"Excuse me for breathing your air," Susannah panted behind me. "I thought you wanted to do some detective work with me, but seeing you'd rather shop for your precious boots—"

"Shut up," I snarled, and she did. I slowed my pace to let her join me. "Where do we start?" I asked as if nothing had happened.

We started with the pet store on the corner, where Susannah of course gave old Beelzebub a good petting (I could almost swear he purred) while I questioned the owner. Sure, he remembered Mr. Withers hobbling by. No, he'd never seen anyone but Juliet with him. All down the street, block after block, it was the same story. People remembered seeing the old man with the silver cane, but always alone or with the little girl with the scar on her cheek.

So finally we reached the bus station.

"Guess this is the end of the line," I said to Susannah.

Little did we know.

I was dying for something cool to drink, so we went into the bus station snack bar. It was lunch time and the place was packed.

"Boy, do I need a drink," I groaned, trying to flag down the waitress as she charged by. "A root beer," I explained to the startled woman on the next stool, and she looked relieved. Then she wanted to know all about us: Were we traveling alone, where were we going, where did we live?

"Oh, we live together," I said airily. "We're sisters."

The woman gawked at Susannah's chocolate face and back at my vanilla one. "Sisters?"

"Uh—sister, old buddy," Susannah hissed in my ear, "I just remembered. I'm broke."

"Never mind, I've got my boot money. We can even have hamburgers. Miss, could we have—?"

The waitress hurtled by like the express to Los Angeles.

"Hey, Josephine!" yelled a fat man down the counter. "Bring some crackers for this soup before it freezes over."

"I've only got two hands!" snapped the waitress as she dumped a pair of sandwiches at our neighbors.

"Two hamburgers and root beers!" I yelled as she raced back with a tray of dirty dishes, but she pretended not to hear. "I hope she drops the tray," I muttered.

She did. The fat man yelped with laughter and somebody down the counter hooted, "Clumsy!" And the next thing I knew, Susannah was around the counter picking up dishes. The waitress barely glanced at her, then raced off to give the fat man his crackers and a very angry woman her cup of tea.

"She didn't even say thanks," I said as Susannah came back around the counter to join me. "See what you get for being nice?"

Zipping past, the waitress spilled two shakes and chocolate pie at us.

"Hey, this isn't what we ordered!" I objected.

"Shut up and eat it," snarled the waitress. "The treat's on me." She shot off again.

I shut up and ate. We polished our plates.

"Want a refill?" The waitress stopped in front of us as I chased my straw after the last bubble in my glass.

The snack bar had emptied when the loudspeaker announced buses to Los Angeles and Reno. Planting her elbows on the counter, the waitress wriggled and sighed contentedly as something snapped in her back. "Rough day. My partner took sick, so I've been trying to handle these hungry hyenas alone. Thanks for the help." She kneaded Susannah's shoulder. "Where you two going?"

"Home," said Susannah. "We live here in town. We just stopped in for a snack."

"I might have known." The waitress shook her head as if remembering something pleasant. "Funny, the nicest people I meet live right here in town. Hey, sugar, what's so funny about that?"

I wasn't laughing at her but the loudspeaker, which had just called for Mr. Bumper and Mr. Plowman.

"Those names," I giggled. "Can't you just see Mr. Bumper running into everybody? And Mr. Plowman pushing a plough to the bus? And that Mrs. Goop they're calling, she sounds like a blob of bubble gum."

They didn't see the humor. In fact, Susannah frowned and poked her glasses down her nose the way she does when she's solving math problems.

"I hadn't thought of that," she muttered. "Yes, of course. If you didn't know that Plowman was a name, you might think it meant a farmer. Now I wonder if . . ."

The waitress—Josephine was the name on her badge—was still going on about what wonderful people lived here. "Like this sweet old guy who used to come in for coffee. I told him all my troubles. Looked so poor I begged him to forget the tip, but he always left me half a dollar."

"Nice guy," I murmured, squirming off my seat. I can only sit so long, especially when I'm bored. "Well, thanks for the pie and shakes, Josephine. We got to go now."

I don't know what made me stop. Maybe it was the alert look on Susannah's face. Maybe it was Josephine's next words: "That sweet old guy. I miss him. I heard he died on the bus back from Sacramento two weeks ago."

Or maybe I'd just realized that the nickname for Josephine is Jo.

Eleven

"WITHERS—was that his name?" Susannah spoke so calmly I could have screamed.

The waitress blinked. "How come you know?" She stared at me. "Hey, you aren't that sweet grandchild he was always talking about—Juliet?"

"Juliet's our friend," I said, so excited that I knocked over my empty glass. "And we've been hunting everywhere for you—Joe."

"Yeah?" Jo looked surprised.

Susannah leaned over the counter. "Listen, Jo—they call you Jo, don't they?—did Mr. Withers ever say anything about a will?"

"Yeah, he talked all the time about his will, honey, but there wasn't nothing in it for little Juliet. That like to have worried him to death, too." Jo's mouth twisted bitterly. "Seems he had to leave everything to some rich niece for some reason. Isn't that always the way?"

"But did he say what he *wanted* to leave Juliet?" I demanded, bouncing on my stool.

"Well, I never got that straight. In fact, you'd never think to look at him that he had so much as a cockroach to leave anybody. Only—"

"Only what?" Susannah and I chorused.

"Well, I just can't believe he'd lie. He wasn't that kind. And he wasn't crazy either—senile, they call it."

"He wasn't lying, Jo." Susannah explained what we knew. "But we think he made another will, and maybe you can help. Did you see him that Friday, two weeks ago, the day he died?"

Jo nodded. "Yeah, but I didn't have time to talk. He came in during rush hour."

"Think carefully, Jo," said Susannah. "You were the last person he knew who saw him. What did he say?"

Jo thought hard. "Well, he told me he was going to Sacramento. Then he said, 'Jo, I've found a way! I've found a way!' I don't know what he meant because I had to go pick up my orders."

Susannah slapped the counter. "I thought so!"

"Thought what?" Then I understood. "You mean he'd found a way to change his will."

"What else? Remember, the day before, he'd asked

Mr. Philips to read his will to him. And Mr. Philips says Mr. Withers acted very pleased with it."

"I don't see why he was pleased, if the will didn't leave Juliet anything."

"What pleased him was the thing that made Mr. Philips want to rewrite the will in proper legal words: There was a loophole in the will."

"Loophole?"

"Come on, Lucy, you're an expert on loopholes. Remember the one you found in the teacher's rule about no candy or gum in class?"

"She never said a word about sunflower seeds," I grumbled. "But she kept me after school anyway."

"Well, in court, loopholes count sometimes," said Susannah. "And Mr. Withers found one that let him leave something to Juliet and still keep his promise to Ivy Withers."

"How could he?" I said. "He promised Ivy the house, and that's all he had."

"Yes, but think how he wrote his will: 'I leave my house to Ivy Withers.' Don't you see the loophole?"

While I pondered, Jo came back from serving a customer.

"Just one other thing, Jo," said Susannah. "Did Mr. Withers say *why* he was going to Sacramento?"

"No," said Jo. "Just that he was going to see some man there. A good man, he called him."

A shiver rippled my scalp. The Good Man again!

Susannah gazed at Jo. "Can you remember his exact words? Pretend you're Mr. Withers and I'm you."

Jo rubbed her chin doubtfully. "Just what I told you. I asked why he was here so early, and he said, 'I'm going to Sacramento to see a good man, Jo.' Then he said he'd found a way, like I told you before, but the cook was yelling for me to pick up my orders and—"

"So he said it like this—pretend I'm Mr. Withers now—'I'm going to Sacramento to see a good man, Jo.' Just like that?"

"Yeah, pretty much. Only he stuttered a bit, he was so excited, see. Like: 'I—I'm g—going to S—Sacramento to see—see a good m—man.'"

"Oh." Susannah twisted her lower lip. "Yes, that makes more sense." She repeated the words, with the stutters, over and over to herself.

"She gets like this." I shrugged at Jo. "But was that all he told you? You never talked to him again?"

Jo shook her head. "By the time I had a moment to talk, he and that lady were leaving."

"WHAT lady?" Susannah jerked out of her reverie.

"The lady who sat down beside him," said Jo. "Didn't I tell you? I was so glad he had somebody nice to talk to while I was busy."

"Did he know her?"

"Well, I think so," said Jo. "They sure got a friendly conversation going fast."

"What did she look like?" asked Susannah. "Young, old, fat, thin?"

"Oh, middling. Not what you'd call young and not what I'd call old. About my age and size, but dressed real expensively. Didn't look like she'd ever worked hard for her living—not in that fancy outfit."

Susannah and I exchanged an excited look.

"I don't suppose you heard any of their conversation?" Susannah asked.

"Just the lady talking about the high price of repairing stuff when I refilled their cups, that's all. She left right after that and he went to catch his bus." She twisted her lip and scoured a stain on the counter. "And I clean forgot to give him that sandwich I fixed for him to take. Wonder if he ever got any lunch?"

Now it was Susannah who couldn't wait to leave. She thanked Jo warmly. "You've been a big help, Jo. I can see why Mr. Withers liked you so much."

In the station concourse people were still dozing, reading and staring at other people squeezing baggage in and out the door, while the loudspeaker sputtered. I hustled to catch up with Susannah.

"You hear that?" I panted. "What Jo said about that woman—a rich lady, she said. You thinking what I'm thinking?"

"I'm just thinking," said Susannah. "Mainly about that Good Man. We've got to talk to him."

"How? All we know is that Mr. Withers went to see some 'good man.' That could be anybody."

"No," said Susannah. "He didn't say: 'I'm going to see a good man.' His exact words were: 'I'm going to *see—see a good man.*' There's a difference."

"So Mr. Withers stuttered. So what?" The loudspeaker, calling Mr. Littleman, caught my attention. "Mr. Littleman! He's probably seven foot ten and weighs a ton."

"Oh, stop it, you name freak." Susannah grinned, then added soberly, "But I can't complain. You've given me the real clue to the Good Man's identity. How much change do you have on you?"

I fumbled in my pocket. "What do you need change for?"

"A call to Sacramento." Susannah dragged me toward the row of phone booths.

"Who're you going to call?"

"A lawyer," said Susannah. "A lawyer named Goodman. Mr. C. A. Goodman, if I'm not mistaken."

Twelve

As it turned out, C. A. Goodman wasn't a good man at all. But she certainly was a nice woman.

"I had no way of knowing Mr. Withers had died before reaching home to tell the Travises about the new will," Miss Goodman explained over coffee in the Higginses' living room two days later. She had arrived that morning to read the new will to the heirs, Ivy Withers and Juliet Travis. Susannah and I had come back from school to find her alone with Judge and Mrs. Higgins. "If it hadn't been for these clever young detectives . . ."

I blushed and squirmed. "I still don't see why Mr. Withers went all the way to Sacramento to find a lawyer," I said, to hide my embarrassment. "Why didn't he just ask Mr. Philips to change the will?"

"I can guess." Judge Higgins stroked his white

mustache. "Philips is a friend of Ivy Withers. The old man was probably embarrassed to ask him to change the will in someone else's favor. And he couldn't go to another lawyer around here without Philips' getting wind of it."

Susannah nodded. "He didn't want to hurt anyone's feelings. Juliet says he was like that."

"Yes, that's the reason he gave me," said Miss Goodman. "So he picked my name out of the Sacramento phone book. And after all his trouble, I doubt his niece even cares. She got the valuable part: the house and the lot it stands on."

Mr. Withers had kept his promise to Ivy and willed her the house. But he had never actually promised her the *contents* of the house. That, as Susannah had guessed, was the loophole in the first will, which Mr. Philips wanted to fix by changing the words "I leave my house to Ivy Withers," to "I leave my house *and its contents* to Ivy Withers." But instead of letting Mr. Philips make the change, Mr. Withers had written a new will, leaving the contents of the house to Juliet.

Not that it mattered much. As Judge Higgins said, "I doubt poor little Juliet and her mother will get more than a couple of hundred dollars from a used furniture dealer."

I couldn't help feeling disappointed that, after all the mystery, we'd ended up with nothing but a pile of

96

junk. Glancing at Susannah's brooding face, I guessed she was disgusted, too. I should have known better.

"Come on," she hissed, towing me up the stairs almost before Miss Goodman was out the front door. "We've got to move fast."

"Huh?" I stumbled behind her.

"The books, Lucy, the books. We've got to find out if any of those in Mr. Withers' library is worth a fortune. Remember that list of history books we wrote down that night?"

She pushed me into a chair at her grandfather's typewriter. "Now make it look businesslike. We don't want them to guess we're kids, or they may not bother with us."

First she wrote out the letter by hand, then I copied it on the typewriter. It took a dozen tries before I got it to suit her. But when we were done, I bet Cross & Evans, Book Dealers, never suspected that the S. J. Higgins who signed the letter was younger than thirty. Then I had to type the whole list of books to send with the letter.

It was almost suppertime when we dropped the letter into the mailbox. Now there was nothing to do but wait.

The next day at school was the best I'd had since the time Knievel Jones missed me and hit the principal with a rubber band. The morning paper had the story about our finding Miss Goodman and the will. It was on the class bulletin board when we arrived, and the principal pinned up another copy downstairs under the words: Our Students Know How To Think. He gave me a baffled look every time we passed.

The only person who didn't treat me with respect that day was, of course, Knievel Jones. He was even nastier than usual, and no wonder, with those dark circles under his eyes. That's what you get, I thought, for staying up to watch the late movies.

Juliet didn't act nearly as pleased as I expected. At first I thought she was still hurt I'd turned up at school looking well after leaving her party sick. But it turned out she just didn't like being the center of attention. "Everybody thinks I'm rich now," she moaned as she and her new friend squeezed in beside us at the lunch table. "They keep asking when I'm going to move into a big house with a swimming pool."

But by the next day things were back to normal. Everybody lost interest in pressing Susannah and me for details of our adventures. And when after a week there was still no answer from the book dealer, I began to lose interest in the case myself. Besides, with basketball season on, I was too busy practicing my shots to think about it.

But one day after school Susannah pulled me into

the backyard of the Blue House and up to the cellar door, almost hidden in overgrown bushes. After a brief examination, she pushed it open.

"Just as I thought." She pointed to the fresh scars on the lock and the doorframe. "That's how our intruder got in—jimmied the lock, of course."

I yanked out a hair, as she asked, and watched her tape one end to the door and the other to the frame.

"What good will that do?"

"Just tell us next time if anybody's opened this door. The prowler won't notice the hair, but it will break if anybody opens the door."

"But suppose the prowler's been back since we were here, and stolen the book already?"

"I don't think so," said Susannah. "Nobody's been in the Withers house since that night we were there, so our operative says."

"Our WHAT?"

"Operative. You know, a lookout, spy. If you're going to be a detective, Lucy, you'd better learn the language."

"Yeah, but *who*'s our operative?"

"It's interesting," Susannah mused as if deaf, "that Ivy Withers has been out of town almost this whole time."

"Susannah," I insisted, "who's our operative?" I had a nasty feeling I knew.

100

And speak of the devil, just then I heard a familiar *Vroom! Vroom!*—the sound Knievel Jones makes when he's being a motorcycle daredevil—and a cat tore past me and dived into the hedge. I dragged Susannah from the sidewalk just in time.

"You crazy nut!" I yelled as his bicycle careened around the corner and squealed to a stop. "Can't you kill yourself on the street without messing up the sidewalk?"

Knievel curled his lip, then turned to Susannah. "Hey, how come I didn't get my name in the paper, too? You said I was a partner in your detective agency."

"Partner!" I bellowed.

"You two are holding out on me," Knievel snarled. "I do all the dirty work and you get the glory. I've been watching that house every night for so long, I've forgotten what TV looks like. Either I get some of the action, or you can just find another op— whatever you call it."

Susannah's great brown eyes pleaded with me. "Fair's fair, Lucy. He *has* been doing the dirty work."

"So?" I tossed my head and turned my back while she told Knievel everything we knew.

"And I swear, Knievel," she finished, "if there's any more investigating to do, you'll be in on it."

He had to be satisfied with that, so with a last suspicious glance, the two-wheeled terror of California mounted and tore off.

"What'd you have to let that creep in on this for?" I sulked.

"Because we need him," said Susannah. "He's the only one who can watch the house. He might be useful in other ways, too. Besides, he knows too much. If he ever tells about us being in the house, we're in trouble."

"Well, I won't be partners with him."

"Don't worry," said Susannah. "This case will be finished when we hear from the book dealer."

She was wrong. Three days later the letter came from the book dealer: None of the books was worth more than twenty dollars.

"What a waste of time," I groaned. "Well, too bad for Juliet. That crazy old man just left her a pile of junk."

Susannah shook her head. "No. I'm sure there's something very valuable in that house."

"Go on," I snorted. "You just *want* to believe that."

"No, I believe it because somebody else does." Susannah peered at me over her glasses. "The prowler."

Thirteen

"WE'VE JUST GOT to get into the Blue House again." Susannah brooded. "Even for an hour or— OUCH!"

"Will you hold still?"

I was corn-rowing her hair in dozens of tiny braids, like the picture in the magazine, and feeling guilty about leaving Pop to eat all alone. Though he said on the phone he didn't mind since it was Friday night and Mrs. Higgins had invited me to dinner and to sleep over. "Even if we *do* get in," I said, "what do we look for?"

"I don't know," Susannah sighed, pushing her glasses down her nose. "Our only clue is the book Mr. Withers told Juliet about. Some kind of history book."

"But there wasn't a thing hidden in any of the history books," I said, "and the book dealer said . . ." I paused, waving the comb in the air.

"Got an idea?"

"No," I snapped, braiding furiously. I'd just had the thought that maybe Pop *wasn't* eating alone. He sure hadn't sounded lonesome on the telephone.

Susannah's shoulders slumped. "Well, I still wish Juliet could remember the title of—OWEEE! How can I think with you scalping me?"

"Look," I growled, "do you want to look like that African model or not?"

"Not," Susannah decided, taking the comb from me. "I told you, I'm not cut out to be a model. Anyway, I bet she doesn't try to solve mysteries while having her hair done. Or maybe she has a better hairdresser."

"Forget you then!" I stalked off but couldn't resist glancing wistfully at the magazine picture and wondering how my straggly yellow hair would look in dozens of braids. Not too great, I decided. "And forget about finding anything but junk furniture in that house, either. And don't tell me *that's* valuable, because it isn't even old. Looks like he made most of it himself, or tried to."

"It looks pretty awful," Susannah agreed. "But the prowler was hunting *something.* Think of the risk he's taking coming back night after night. Lucy, we've just got to find it before the prowler does."

"What are we waiting for? We know where the spare key is."

Susannah squirmed. "I hate sneaking back in there again. I wish we had an excuse for asking Mrs. Travis to let us in without telling her the real reason."

"So we just sit around doing nothing while Mrs. Travis sells everything to the junk dealers?"

"No, we don't just do nothing," Susannah said. "We try to discover who was the mysterious woman Mr. Withers met in the bus station."

Jo promised to meet us the next afternoon, a Saturday, when she finished her shift.

"And just what do we say to Ivy Withers when we knock on her door?" I asked Susannah as we walked to the bus station. "'Excuse me, ma'am, Jo just wants to see if you're the lady who was with Mr. Withers in the bus station?'"

"That"—Susannah grinned—"wouldn't be cool. No, we'll say, 'Would you like to buy a raffle ticket to help the children's clinic, Miss Withers?'" She flashed a handful of green tickets at me. "Who knows? We might even sell some."

We met Jo, grabbed a bus, and twenty minutes later got off near Ivy Withers' house.

It didn't take a detective to deduce that she was having a party. The circular driveway was filled with

cars, while others squirmed into the nearest spaces in front and people hurried up the walk. One of the guests reached the door just as we did.

"Hello, Mr. Philips," said Susannah.

It took him a minute to answer. "Oh yes, Judge Higgins' niece, Samantha."

"Granddaughter, and Susannah," she replied unperturbed. "We're selling raffle tickets."

That was my cue. "Only a dollar to win a brand new quadraphonic, ultra—ugh!" Susannah poked my ribs.

"You probably aren't interested, Mr. Philips," Susannah said quickly, "but maybe Miss Withers will help us out. It's for a very good cause."

Before Mr. Philips could get his wallet out of his pocket, the door opened and Susannah shoved me in. The hallway was crammed with people and hazy with smoke. Ivy Withers pushed her way toward us.

"John," she simpered. "You made it, after all." She wore one of those dark, shapeless dresses she always wore, probably hoping it made her look thinner. By contrast, Miss Valentine in her red hair and dress to match looked like a neon sign rushing toward us.

"John Philips!" squealed Miss Valentine. "Just the person I want to talk to."

Ivy pumped Jo's hand, saying it was so nice she could come. Apparently she thought she'd invited her. Mr. Philips came to the rescue.

"Ivy, you remember Judge Higgins' granddaughter Sandra. She and her friends are raising money for a very worthy cause—Red Cross, did you say?"

I started my speech about the stereo set, but Ivy cut me off.

"Of course, I'd be happy to buy a raffle ticket. I think it's wonderful you're spending your playtime raising money for a deserving cause."

"So unlike most children today," said Miss Valentine. "Most of them think only about having fun. When I was a child . . ." But she didn't offer to buy a raffle ticket. Not that it mattered, for we sold them all before we left.

I counted our afternoon's take as we walked back to the bus stop. "Sixteen dollars. Not bad, when we weren't really trying to sell them."

"Great," Susannah said absently. "Well, what do you think, Jo? Was that the woman?"

Jo hesitated. "Well, the woman in the bus station was dressed different. Her hair was different, too. It's hard to say."

My enthusiasm left me. Had all this been for nothing?

Jo made up her mind. "I'm not positive, mind, but I think that *was* the lady."

Fourteen

"SURE, YOU CAN HAVE any books of Grandpa's you want," Juliet said the next morning when we knocked on her door on our way back from Susannah's church.

I'd spent most of my morning in Sunday school trying to think up a good excuse for getting into the Blue House. For we knew Mrs. Travis had her key back. Ivy Withers returned it when Juliet inherited the furniture. Meantime I'd discovered that the key from the birdhouse was no longer in the mailbox where we'd left it. Probably Ivy had found it there. Now our only chance was to find an excuse to get Mrs. Travis' key.

My time at Sunday school wasn't wasted. The excuse I came up with solved another problem, too: what I was going to write my social studies report about. It could be about anyplace in the world—and I'd thought of just the place.

109

"I'll go right over and get them now." Juliet slipped on a faded jacket. "What are the names of those two books again? Something about Cro—Cro-what?"

"Croatia," I said. "It's part of Yugoslavia now." (I'd done some checking.) "But you'll never find them. Just let us have the key and we'll go hunt them."

Juliet studied us in silence a moment. "You'll have to ask Mom for the key."

Mrs. Travis, as usual, was painting in the dining room.

"Lucy, Susannah! How nice to see you." More than ever we were special guests since finding the will. "Juliet, is there any carrot cake left? And make some fresh mint tea." She set down her glass with a ghastly expression. "That last batch tastes awful."

"I bet it does," Juliet said. "You just washed your brushes in it, Mom."

Mrs. Travis was quite willing to lend me the books, but not so willing to hand over the key.

"I don't like letting anyone in unless I'm there—it's still Ivy Withers' house," she apologized. "I can't go with you now because I have to fix lunch, then go see a used furniture dealer."

"Why don't I take them over after lunch, while you're at the used furniture dealer's?" Juliet suggested. "Miss Withers can't mind *my* going in the house." Mrs. Travis agreed to that.

Back in the kitchen, Susannah said casually, "If you'll just give us the keys, Juliet, you don't have to bother—"

"Forget it, Susannah," said Juliet. "I know you want to search the house. Like you did before, didn't you?"

"How did you know?" I asked weakly.

"Simple. You gave it away when you asked for the books. You couldn't have seen them that time you were with Mom and me—we were only in the library a minute. I bet that's where you were the night of my party."

"Anybody ever tell you you'd make a good detective?" Susannah grinned sheepishly, then confessed everything. "You mad at us?"

"Well, I *was* mad after I realized you weren't really sick when you left my party. But you did it for me, didn't you?" Juliet hugged us both together. She looked pretty when she smiled, I noticed. "But this time I'm going with you. Only please don't be disappointed if whatever Grandpa left me turns out to be nothing very valuable. It's probably just some little thing he thought I'd like."

We promised.

"As long as we're making it a party"—Susannah glanced uneasily at me—"we'd better ask Knievel. We did promise, you know."

"*You* promised," I corrected, half tempted to add

111

that if Knievel was coming, I wasn't. But that wouldn't hurt Knievel's feelings.

"Knievel's coming? Oh good." Juliet looked pleased. "He's nice. He used to beat up kids who made fun of my scar. Our mothers are good friends. They've both been divorced a long time."

We agreed to meet in an hour, and Susannah and I went home for lunch. I was sorry I bothered. At first sniff our kitchen promised a heavenly meal, but as soon as I opened the oven, Pop yelled:

"Leave that alone! That's dinner!"

"Wow!" I breathed the steam. "What's the big occasion?"

I should have known.

"My friend Mae's coming to eat with us tonight."

I swallowed that fact in silence, then turned my back and fixed a tuna sandwich. I was starting out the back door when Pop's voice stopped me.

"Dishes." He pointed to the sink. "Then go clean your room. I don't want Mae thinking we live in a pigpen."

"Oink, oink, sir." I saluted coldly.

Pop didn't smile. "None of your sass, girl. You heard. That room better be decent before you leave this house."

"But Pop . . ." He was gone.

The clock said ten to one. We were meeting at one-thirty. I'd never finish cleaning up in time. It wasn't fair. Well, I had to try. I scooped up the tuna, bread, mayonnaise and milk, shoved them into the refrigerator, then dumped my glass and plate into the sink on top of the breakfast dishes, and turned on the tap. One wipe with the sponge and another with the towel, and I tumbled the dishes into the cupboard. Six minutes gone. I snatched the broom and dustpan and charged down the hall.

All hope left me as I faced the dismal truth of my room. Still, I couldn't give up now. Taking a breath, I rushed into the chaos—and promptly slipped on a marble and slid belly down on a skateboard all the way to the closet before the front wheel got tangled in a yo-yo string just as the back wheel stuck in a wad of bubble gum. Jumping up, I snatched my clothes, baseball equipment, magazines, and pitched them into the closet, then leaned on the door till it scrunched shut. The puzzle pieces and other bits I swept under the bed, tossing the tangled blankets behind, and pulled the bedspread down low to hide the debris. It was going to take weeks to relocate my things, but I couldn't worry about that now.

I was polishing the dresser with my shirttail when Pop arrived for inspection at ten after one. For one uneasy moment I thought he would open the closet or peer under the bed, but he changed his mind.

"Never mind how you did it, speedy." Pop grinned. "It looks okay, so go play now."

I reached the corner just as the 1:14 bus did, and so arrived at the Blue House before the others, after all. It was a good thing, for I needed some time to myself. I wanted to think, and the old porch swing suited my mood. It screeched as I swung, but the sound didn't bother me any more than the jays quarreling in the apricot tree. I watched a spider spin a web while a jay perched on the empty feeder scolded me. I must tell Mrs. Travis to fill the feeder and put some water in the birdbath, I thought.

The mail carrier stopped at the gate. "You startled me, sitting there in the swing," he said. "Old man Withers used to sit right there every day this time. Sure do miss him. He always had a glass of iced tea waiting for me, and we'd pass the time of day awhile."

I think it was at that moment I began to solve what Susannah calls the most important part of this mystery: Mr. Withers himself. Though I wasn't even thinking about the mystery when I realized suddenly that Mr. Withers had been a very happy man.

I'd always pictured him before as lonely and bitter about losing his fortune and precious antiques, hiding in his junk-filled house. A recluse because of his pride, Ivy Withers had said. But that wasn't the way it was at all. He'd found new friends who didn't care whether

114

he was rich or poor. How could he be lonely with Juliet and Mrs. Travis next door, the mail carrier stopping by every afternoon, and if he felt like a walk, Jo at the bus station?

Ivy and Miss Valentine wouldn't understand that, or how a man who'd lost "everything" could be happy just swinging on his porch, watching beetles lumber by and tempting finches to eat from his hand. But I understood.

I was almost in a good mood when Susannah arrived.

"Okay, let's get going. Where are the others?"

Vroom! Vroom! Vroom! Down the street sped the boy daredevil himself on his secondhand bicycle, wheels buzzing with a paper contraption he fondly imagines sounds like a Honda, but reminds me more of a chicken who's laid an egg. He leaped the curb and zoomed up the walk, screeching to a halt almost in time—but not quite; he finished his act on his rump in a weed patch.

"Terrific!" I applauded. "Keep practicing, and when you can land on your head, I'll even buy a ticket to watch."

Knievel picked away the vines from his face. "Your grandmother!" he muttered.

"Yours lives in the zoo," I retorted pleasantly.

"The zoo won't even take yours."

Juliet's arrival interrupted our discussion of ancestors.

"Sorry I'm late," she puffed. "Ivy Withers just came by. We've got to sell the stuff right away, because she has a buyer for the house."

Fifteen

IN THE GLOW OF the afternoon sun through the shades, the musty living room held none of the mystery, the eerie elegance, it had in the dark. It seemed rather pathetic with its sagging, throw-covered sofas and painted blue end tables. Here and there were tall, lumpy chairs in baggy slipcovers.

"Jeez, what junk!" Knievel whistled.

Juliet's face reddened. "Don't talk like that about Grandpa's things. He loved his house." She added bitterly, "I hate the thought of junk dealers pawing over his stuff and making fun of it."

I felt the same. Now that I knew Mr. Withers, so to speak, his house no longer seemed either funny or scary, or even sad. It was part of him. But a part I still didn't quite understand somehow.

"Well, let's get on with it," Susannah said briskly.

117

"Juliet, you go through the books in the library and find the one Mr. Withers told you about. The rest of us will start upstairs."

Knievel and I followed her up the squeaky stairs to the bedroom. I couldn't help feeling glad I wasn't alone, and I let them go in first.

But here, too, everything looked perfectly ordinary in the daylight. Just a large bedroom sparsely furnished with a grotesque bed, an equally ugly bureau and a cheap nightstand. Where had the mystery gone? Where was the demon face that had leered at me from the dark? It had become just a lump in the headboard covered over with Con-Tact paper.

"That's right, Lucy," said Susannah. "Give the bed a good going-over, and don't forget to look under the mattress. Then check the nightstand again, just to be sure. Knievel, you take the bureau." She herself took charge of the closet.

There was nothing under the mattress, and only the things we'd seen before in the nightstand drawer.

"Anything in the bureau, Knievel?" Susannah called from the closet, where she was rapping her knuckles around the walls.

"Sure," Knievel snorted. "Socks, shorts, shirts— what do you expect?" He shoved the drawer back, and it promptly slid halfway out again.

"What I expect," Susannah said as she emerged from the closet, "is to hear about anything I *don't* ex-

118

pect in a bureau. Quit worrying with that drawer—it doesn't fit right—and come help me examine the walls."

She showed us how to search for cracks that might betray a hidden door, and to tap the panels to be sure they were solid. "Don't forget the baseboards," she warned, watching us critically, "and check behind the pictures."

"You really think we're going to find a secret room or something?" Knievel asked.

"No," said Susannah. "But a grand old house like this should have a safe somewhere. They sometimes hid them behind a false panel or under a picture. Or there might be just a small space, say in the baseboard, where you could put a few jewels."

But the bedroom walls seemed solid, so Susannah left us to check the walls of the empty rooms down the hall while she went up to the attic. A few minutes later she returned, brushing a cobweb from her hair.

"Nothing up there but cans of dried blue paint and a trunk of mildewed clothes. Let's try the junk room."

If the rest of the house held nothing but junk furniture, the storeroom was crammed with the worst of it—three-legged tables, chairs without seats, a cordless vacuum cleaner and all sorts of chipped dishes. A thick layer of dust lay over everything.

"Where do we start?" I eyed the clutter with dismay.

"Just follow the path, I think," Susannah said.

Sure enough, a kind of path wound through the crippled furniture and useless appliances. We followed Susannah down it, pausing before an ancient Victrola and an even older radio.

"Poor guy." I pointed out a pile of drawers. "He never bought dressers with drawers that fit right."

"Boy, I bet nobody's been in this room for years," Knievel said.

"Really want to bet? I'd say somebody was here not more than two weeks ago. Look." Susannah pointed to a table, gray under years of dust except for five clear marks where a hand had rested.

I sucked in my breath. "The prowler . . . ?"

"Probably that night we were here," said Susannah. "Remember, you heard somebody going down the hall up here. The person probably heard Knievel crawling through the bedroom window and came here to hide."

"And you said that was just my imagination," I sulked.

"Sorry, my mistake. Hey, look at this!" She pounced on a dusty fishbowl. "A cigarette butt."

I peered at the roll of ash with brown fragments of paper still clinging to it. "Maybe Mr. Withers left it there."

"Not likely," Susannah said. "Mr. Withers didn't smoke."

"Juliet said so?"

120

"She didn't have to. It's obvious. Have you seen an ashtray anywhere in the house? Well, now we know the prowler is somebody who smokes. Wish we could tell what brand it is."

"That *could* be a cigar," said Knievel. "Maybe the paper isn't burnt but was brown to start with. You can't tell now."

"Cigars are fatter than that, you moron," I scoffed, but I saw what he meant.

Susannah studied the ashes. "It's hard to tell now. . . . Well"—she let her glasses slide back down her nose as she stood up—"let's go downstairs."

"But we haven't looked through this junk yet," Knievel protested.

"I think we can save it for later, like the prowler did," said Susannah. "He'd have left fingerprints if he searched in all this dust, so he must have thought it wasn't here."

Downstairs in the library, Juliet sat beside a pile of history books, examining them one by one. The rest of us checked the wall that wasn't covered with books, then Susannah sent Knievel to check the other walls downstairs. He didn't seem to mind. Maybe being around books made him nervous.

Before I forgot, I took the two books about Croatia and wrapped them in my jacket to take home, after showing the covers to Juliet.

"What's next?" I said.

Susannah pulled out the secret drawer, this time without peeling off the false book backs. "Ever seen this before?" She grinned at Juliet.

Juliet stared, open-mouthed.

I groaned. "We've been through all that stuff already."

"But not carefully—only to see if the will was there. This time we're hunting a clue to something valuable. And judging by his bedroom, I think he left a clue somewhere."

"We didn't find any clues in the bedroom," I objected.

"We did in a way," said Susannah. "A clue to the kind of man Mr. Withers was: a very tidy man who kept his personal things in good order. And the storeroom showed us that he never threw anything away, either. So he must have left a clue somewhere."

Sighing dramatically, I took out the envelopes marked Clippings and Important Documents and laid them aside, but Susannah insisted we go through them again. So while she examined warranties for toasters and radios long since sent to the junk room, I scanned articles cut from old newspapers and magazines. Most were from a magazine called *Today's Antiques.* The article about the house caught my eye.

"Susannah, suppose maybe some of the valuable things they talk about here *weren't* stolen, after all?"

Susannah studied the article over my shoulder.

"Where's that newspaper clipping about the robbery?" I shoved it between her fingers, and for a few minutes her head swiveled back and forth from one article to the other.

"No, everything the magazine talks about is listed in the newspaper report of the robbery. Except—what about this clock with the gold angels?"

Juliet looked at the picture. "Oh, that's the one Grandpa sold to Miss Valentine. I remember going with him. It was at the repair shop during the robbery."

I put the articles back into the envelope after a last regretful look at the pictures.

"Nothing here either." Susannah tucked her stack of warranties and yellowed receipts into the Important Documents envelope. "He sure never threw anything away, did he? Now why did he keep this old passport?"

"Maybe to remind him of his trip to Europe," I said.

Susannah flipped through the pages. "He sure went all over—Britain, France, Italy, Yugoslavia—isn't that where your Croatia is?"

I nodded. "I guess that's why he got those books."

There wasn't much left in the drawer but the stack of letters, which Susannah halved with me. I took my share back to the table, or at least, that's where I was heading when my shoe stuck in something.

124

"All right," I bellowed, "who dropped chewing gum on the rug?"

"Chewing gum?" Susannah looked up. "Oh no, not after Mrs. Travis let us—No"—she frowned—"none of us was chewing. Here, let me look at that."

"It's glue," she reported, examining the spot. "Strong glue. Probably the sticky part of epoxy without the hardener."

"But who was using glue? Ivy?"

"Maybe. But why?" She sat on her haunches, peering over her glasses. Then she rose brusquely. "Well, we'll think about it later. Right now, let's finish our investigations."

But the letters held no surprises either. They were business letters, years old and mostly from antique dealers saying they were shipping him this thing or that. It was sad reading them and knowing all the stuff had been stolen later. In fact, one of the letters, from an antique dealer in New York, was dated only two days before the robbery. I showed it to Susannah.

"What a shame," I said. "This stuff must have arrived just in time to be stolen. Mr. Withers didn't even get to—YEEKS!"

I didn't hear Knievel sneak up behind me until his fingers jabbed my ribs.

Susannah pulled us apart. "Stop it, you two. We don't have time for that now. Did you find anything in the other rooms, Knievel?"

"Nothing," he said. "Nothing under the rug, in the drawers, behind the pictures, in the walls or—Ouch!" I'd landed a kick right on his shin. "You dirty sneak, I'll—"

But Susannah has a surprisingly strong right arm, and Knievel found himself pinned against the table as I danced away.

"You had it coming," Susannah told him. "Now make up your mind: Are you going to be a detective or a clown? Because we haven't got time—"

"Okay, okay. I was just play—" He froze.

We all did. For we'd just realized we'd left the front door unlocked.

And somebody was opening that door.

Sixteen

"Yoo-hoo! Juliet?" It was Mrs. Travis.

We grinned at each other foolishly. I don't know who—or what—we'd expected.

Juliet called back, and a moment later her mother poked her head into the library.

"Haven't you found those books yet, Lucy?"

It took me a few seconds to remember that we were supposed to be here to find the books about Croatia.

"I'm sure they're here somewhere," I said lamely. Which was the truth, because they were both wrapped in my jacket.

Before I had to explain what we'd been doing all this time, Miss Valentine appeared in the doorway. When I'd seen her at Judge Higgins' party, her hair had been black; now it was an unlikely shade of red that clashed with the silky pink of her pants suit.

Mrs. Travis made introductions. "Miss Valentine, this is my daughter Juliet. And this is Susannah and Lucy and Knievel."

Miss Valentine simpered, "I've met these young ladies already. And read about them in the newspaper, how they found that second will of John Withers'. Very clever girls indeed. You must be very grateful to them, Mrs. Travis."

"I am," Mrs. Travis said warmly. Though I wondered what she really had to be grateful for. Thanks to us, here she was trying to be a sensible businesswoman instead of doing her painting. And at best, she might sell the furniture for enough to cover a couple months' rent.

"You were right, there's nothing but junk here," Miss Valentine said. "It's hard to believe if you'd ever seen this room in the old days. Then there were Persian carpets, two-hundred-year-old English chairs, and such an elegant little eighteenth century French desk where that monstrosity—" She looked at the long table and shuddered.

Mrs. Travis pressed her lips together. "I'm sorry you wasted your time coming. Shall we go?"

"I might as well look upstairs as long as I'm here." Miss Valentine's eyes swept over the room again. "And I suppose I *could* use that awful table in my workroom. I need something I don't have to worry about spilling varnish or stain on."

"I was thinking of keeping it myself," said Mrs. Travis. "It would be perfect for mixing paints on, instead of ruining my dining table."

Miss Valentine shrugged. "I'm sure I can find a suitable worktable elsewhere. Shall we go upstairs now?"

The door closed behind them, and we listened to their squeaking steps up the stairs: the *clunk-clunk* of Mrs. Travis' health-store sandals and the mincing click of Miss Valentine's gold strapless shoes.

Susannah broke the silence. "Juliet," she whispered fiercely, "don't let your mother sell *anything*. And keep them upstairs as long as you can." Juliet nodded and slipped out the door.

"If we only had more time." Susannah sucked in her breath. "If Juliet could find that book or we could find the safe."

"But we've looked everywhere," I said.

The uncomfortable look on Knievel's face made me suddenly suspicious. "Knievel, you did check *all* the walls?"

He squirmed. "Well, all but two in the living room. Look, my knuckles are bleeding. I came back to tell you it's time you took some skin off yours."

"Cool it." Susannah glared at me before I could think up something really nasty to say. "Knievel's done his share."

There was no time to waste—the clatter of high

heels over our heads told us Miss Valentine had seen enough of the bedroom and was heading for the junk room.

The FBI couldn't have searched the living room more thoroughly in five minutes. We tapped the walls and peeked behind pictures. We even rolled back the rugs, but all we found there was another faded rug underneath, apparently to pad the thin one on top.

"I give up," I groaned, dropping onto a rickety chair.

"Me too." Knievel pushed aside a small lamp and sat down on an end table covered with a tablecloth. At least, it looked like it was supposed to be an end table.

There was a rip, a loud crack of wood splintering, and Knievel's bottom disappeared.

"Get me out of here!" he yelped, kicking wildly.

Susannah and I ran to pull him out. Well okay, so I didn't exactly run. Was it my fault I was laughing so hard I couldn't straighten up? As we hauled him out, I was trying to think of a funny remark about why end tables were called end tables, when I heard Susannah gasp:

"The safe!"

Sure enough, there it was: a small iron safe under the tablecloth and flimsy wood split by Knievel's weight.

"Nice detective work." Susannah grinned at Knievel.

"Yeah," I said, "I always knew he must have brains *some*where."

Knievel rubbed the back of his pants and said, "Shut up."

There was a tattoo of heels on the stairs and Miss Valentine's voice: "Thanks for showing me around, dear. I will take that awful bed off your hands, as I said. It's not much, but a cousin of mine needs something cheap. I'm sure you won't get a better offer. And I might go a little bit higher on the library table—it does seem sturdy enough. Think about it."

"I will," Mrs. Travis said, "and if we don't get a better offer— What are you children doing here?"

"Nothing," I said, and Susannah and Knievel said they weren't doing anything either.

"Well, suppose you go do nothing at home. This is Ivy Withers' house, and frankly, I don't feel right letting you play in it."

"Coming," I said, without moving from in front of the safe.

"Right now," Susannah added, pressing closer to me.

"Me too," said Knievel, trying not to sink back into the hole over which he was perched.

Juliet read the desperate look on our faces and somehow got her mother and Miss Valentine out the door by promising we'd leave right away. Before their voices had faded down the walk, we had cleared the tablecloth and slats from the safe.

"But how do we get it open?" I demanded. "We don't know the combination and we haven't got a stick of dynamite—oh," I finished as Knievel pulled the door open. Which didn't take much genius. The lock was broken.

I held my breath as the heavy door of the safe swung back. Would there be jewels or stacks of money inside or . . . ?

There was nothing but a dozen faded snapshots.

Susannah shuffled through them, her face showing her disappointment. They were pictures of a man about Pop's age but dressed in clothes my grandfather might have worn when he was young. The man was faintly familiar, and I realized he must be Mr. Withers. The snapshots showed him posed by a fountain in a garden, in a doorway with a long dining-room table and chairs behind, and leaning on various pieces of furniture.

"Is this all?" Susannah put the pictures back in the safe. "I was sure there'd be a key."

Seventeen

"WHAT KEY?" I muttered at Susannah's back as we four trudged out the front door of the Blue House.

"Later," Susannah muttered back, as Mrs. Travis locked the door behind us.

She led us toward Juliet's apartment. Going through the gap in the hedge, I caught my jacket on a briar and dropped one of the books I was carrying. It sprawled open on the path.

Juliet picked it up. "You dropped your b— . . . Oh!" she finished in an astonished whisper.

We all stopped and stared at her. Juliet gazed at *Historical Mansions of Croatia* as if she couldn't believe it.

"This is it! This is the book Grandpa showed me. I remember the pictures."

"But I asked you before I took it," I protested.

"There in the library, remember? You said you'd never seen it before."

"I didn't remember the name. But the pictures—"

Susannah took the book from Juliet and, sitting on the Travis' kitchen steps, painstakingly examined it. She peered down the spine, checked the covers and endpapers for lumps, then scrutinized every page. Nothing.

"Not so much as a word underlined," she sighed, passing the book to me. "Strange. We know it's not a valuable, rare book, so what . . . ?"

"Maybe if we tore off the binding—" I suggested.

"No you don't." Juliet took the book and clasped it to her chest. "You're not tearing up the book Grandpa left me."

"I've got a feeling we're on the wrong track anyway." Susannah opened the door to the kitchen. "I think it's time for our detective agency to hold its first meeting and discuss the clues in this case."

"What clues?" Knievel scoffed as we took our places around the kitchen table. "We don't have any clues."

"No clues?" Susannah stared at him over her glasses. "Juliet's book, the glue on the library rug, the lady in the bus station, the ashes in the fishbowl— You don't call those clues?"

"What I want to know," I said, "is about that key. The one you thought would be in the safe."

"Yes, that's interesting." Susannah pushed her

glasses down to the tip of her nose. "The key. It wasn't in the secret drawer, so I was sure he'd hidden it in the safe, but it wasn't there either. So—"

"*What* key?" I demanded.

"Why, the key to a safe-deposit box in a bank, of course." Susannah looked at me as if I'd turned into an idiot. "People usually put their valuable papers and jewelry and things in a safe-deposit box."

"Well, where *is* the key?" asked Knievel.

Susannah shrugged. "There isn't one. That's my guess, anyway. He didn't have a safe-deposit box. But in that case, the question is: Why didn't he have one?"

I was thinking hard. "Why not? He could have put whatever-it-is in a safe-deposit box and willed the contents to Juliet. That way he wouldn't have to fool around with all that business about making a second will. It doesn't make sense."

"Oh, but it *does* make sense." Susannah smiled. "There's a good reason why he couldn't put this thing in a safe-deposit box. Think, Lucy."

I pondered. I'd never seen a safe-deposit box, but I knew it was a locked drawer in the vault of a bank. A perfect place to hide things—except—except—

I snapped my fingers. "You can't put anything very big in a safe-deposit box!"

"Right!" Susannah slapped my palm and I slapped back. "So we know we're looking for something large. Not jewelry or money or stuff like that."

136

Juliet looked up from *Historical Mansions of Croatia*. She still hadn't put the book down. "What difference does it make how big it is?"

"A lot," said Susannah. "It's hard to hide something large. In fact . . ." She frowned over her glasses in that way I knew well. "In fact, maybe the best way would be . . ."

"What?" I prompted after a silence. "Where do you think he hid it?"

"The question," Susannah said slowly, "isn't *where*, but *how* he hid it. Think now, how would Mr. Withers hide something large?"

Knievel shrugged. "Who knows what that crazy old man would do? Look how he hid that silly safe with nothing worth having in it."

"I *am* thinking of the safe," said Susannah, "and about the secret drawer in the bookcase. They're the clues. They tell us how Mr. Withers hid large things. Don't you see?"

Knievel and I saw at the same time. "He made them look like—"

"—like something else!"

I groaned. "I might have known. Nothing in this case has been what it seemed. The mystery man Joe turns out to be a nice waitress, the 'good man' is a lady lawyer—"

"And what looks like a good place to sit down has an iron safe underneath." Knievel rubbed his bottom.

"Anyway, the 'treasure' is probably still in the house," said Susannah. "Even if the prowler's found it by now, it's too big to sneak out."

"That explains why he hasn't been back," said Knievel. "He's still waiting for his chance to take it."

I jumped up. "What are we waiting for? Let's go find it."

Susannah motioned me to sit down. "Before we wreck the house, looking in the wrong places for something we may not know when we see it, let's finish examining the clues."

I sat down. "What clues?"

"This book, for one thing." Susannah plucked it from Juliet's hands and laid it open on the table before her. The pages, as always, fanned apart at the place near the end. "It's the one clue Mr. Withers left us himself."

"But there's nothing in that book," I argued. "We practically took it apart."

"We must have missed something," Susannah muttered. But after thumbing the pages and rubbing the inside covers for telltale lumps, she put the book down with a sigh and was about to return it to Juliet when she suddenly uttered a most un-Susannah-like squeak. "Great galloping gophers!" she whispered, staring at the sprawling pages.

Since that's as close to swearing as Susannah ever comes, I sat up. "What's the matter?"

She gaped at the open pages as if she'd never seen them before. "I'm an idiot!" She slapped her forehead. "Here I've been busy hunting secret messages and never noticed what's plain for any half-wit to see."

"What?" said Knievel as if he'd heard his name called.

"Don't you see?" Susannah pointed to the open pages. "When you have a favorite book—and this must have been Mr. Withers' favorite—there's always some part you like best. You turn to it so often that pretty soon the pages just naturally open there."

"You mean there's something special about these pages?" I peered at them curiously over her shoulder, wondering what I'd missed all the times I'd seen them. They certainly didn't look interesting. The left-hand page was all small print, and on the right side were pictures plainly taken a long time ago, for the women wore long dresses, the kind you see in TV westerns, and the men seemed to be choking on high collars. One picture showed these uncomfortably dressed people around a long, laden dining table. It reminded me of something, but I couldn't think what.

I read aloud from the printed page: " 'That afternoon his brother called on the count to discuss this state of affairs. They agreed to continue their opposition to the compromise with Hungary. On Monday the count gave a reception, his guests including—' " I skipped over the names. " 'Next day about eleven

o'clock a messenger arrived from Dal—Dalmatia—'"

"Oh, dry up," Knievel interrupted. "We can read."

"Yeah?" I said dubiously.

"Stop it, you two," Susannah ordered, glaring over her glasses. "It's time to get moving now. Juliet, get the key to the Blue House— Yes, we *do* have to get in, and right away. Knievel, you bring Mrs. Travis' toolbox."

"Toolbox?"

"Yes, toolbox," she repeated impatiently. "I've just realized why there was glue on the library rug. And Lucy, you phone some long-distance truckers. Look them up in the phone book. Ask how long it takes to ship things from here in California back to New York."

"Why?" I asked, reaching for the phone book.

"Because I was wrong. The book isn't the only clue Mr. Withers left us. Remember that letter in the secret drawer—the one you showed me? Now I understand what didn't make sense about it."

Eighteen

WHEN KNIEVEL AND I arrived, lugging the toolbox between us, we found Susannah in the library, crawling under the table while Juliet held the lamp down for her to see.

"Uh huh!" Susannah grunted and backed out. "Just as I thought. And here's something our prowler forgot to glue back."

I squinted at the sliver of wood in her hand. "So? What's the big deal about a splinter?"

Susannah stared at each of us in turn. "Don't you see?"

I glanced at the others. "No, we don't."

"But you saw the book . . . that page it opens to," Susannah said plaintively.

"So?" Knievel shrugged. "What's all that garbage

about some old count and his brother got to do with Juliet's fortune?"

Susannah groaned. "Not *that* page, you dummies. The other one—the pictures." She snatched the book from the table, where it lay open. "Look at those pictures. *Now* do you see?"

I saw what I'd seen before: two women with high hairdos and long skirts posing in a garden, a stiff-collared man in front of a painting, and following Susannah's finger, a dozen or so people seated around a long table piled with dishes and food. I gazed at this last picture while a strange excitement crept up the back of my head.

"You mean—?" Speechless, I pointed to the spot her finger was tapping. I realized why this picture reminded me of a snapshot in Mr. Withers' safe.

"Well, of course, what else?" Susannah sighed. "I should have realized all along there's only one kind of treasure Mr. Withers would have."

"But it *can't* be the same one," I sputtered. "Not this awful-looking thing."

"We'll soon find out," said Susannah. "The same way our prowler did. Get a hammer and chisel out of the toolbox."

Knievel still didn't get it. "You mean that necklace the lady in the picture has on? What's that got to do with a splinter?"

"Nothing," I said, raking through the toolbox, which wasn't any neater than you'd expect Mrs. Travis' toolbox to be. "Forget the necklace. In fact, forget the people. Take them out of the picture and see what's left."

He saw it fast enough then and was soon scrabbling through the toolbox with me. We found the chisel at the same moment and were wrestling for it when—

"Hush!" Susannah ordered.

Heavy footsteps were coming down the hall.

"What are you children doing here?" demanded Mr. Philips.

"Who let you in?" Ivy Withers tried to look stern, but she couldn't have scared an earthworm.

"I did," Juliet said coolly. "We wanted to look through Grandpa's books—*my* books, I mean." She didn't need to add that she had a right to do so; they got the point.

"You kids shouldn't be alone in an empty house," was all Mr. Philips could grumble. "It isn't safe."

"No, it isn't," Susannah said pointedly. "You never know if some burglar might be hiding upstairs."

Mr. Philips made a sound that could have been a cough. Ivy frowned. I wondered if he pulled at his collar because it was too tight, or if it was Ivy's girdle that made her squirm.

Mr. Philips cleared his throat. "We'd like to examine this room, if it's all the same to you." His sarcasm plainly meant that we were supposed to scram, but we ignored the hint. "Miss Withers wants to see if any repairs are necessary before she can sell the house. This *is* her property, you know."

"Now, John," Ivy murmured reprovingly.

I felt like asking Mr. High-and-Mighty if he'd smoked any good cigars lately, and Knievel looked ready to make a few choice remarks of his own. But Susannah's look warned us to keep quiet. She glanced pointedly at the end of the toolbox poking out from under the chair, where we'd shoved it when we heard them coming. It was too late to hide it now, so I simply sat down in front of it and hoped.

Mr. Philips and Ivy Withers passed by us and around the long table to the narrow window that faced a small weed patch and the kitchen wall. While they stood there discussing drains and waterspouts, Susannah picked up the open book from the table and motioned us to do the same. We each dutifully grabbed a book from the shelves and for the next ten minutes, as we waited desperately for our unwelcome visitors to leave, we read in a silence that would have burst the school librarian's ears—if her heart was strong enough to survive the shock of seeing Knievel Jones buried in a book. (She'd have been even more surprised to discover that his book was in French.)

At last the two at the window turned around.

"I suppose I have to do something about the roof," Ivy was saying. "Uncle said it leaked the last time I saw him."

I nearly dropped my book at hearing Ivy give herself away. Of course, she didn't know that Jo had heard her talking with Mr. Withers about making repairs that last day in the bus station.

"When was that, Ivy?" Mr. Philips asked curiously.

At that moment I, like a fool, dropped the chisel. Everyone jumped.

"What's this?" Mr. Philips dived for the chisel so fast we nearly bumped heads, but he had it first. As he rose, he noticed the toolbox poking out from under the chair. He tapped it with his toe. "You kids aren't planning to dismantle the house, are you?"

While I stammered for an answer, Susannah replied calmly: "We thought we'd try to repair a piece of Juliet's furniture. Looks like someone tried to take it apart."

Mr. Philips shrugged. "Just don't practice your carpentry on that table, will you? It may be an eyesore, but I'm planning to buy it from Mrs. Travis. I need a sturdy long table for my workroom."

Ivy frowned. "Surely you can find another table. It's just the right size for my greenhouse, and I've already spoken to Mrs. Travis—"

"Now look, Ivy—"

146

"John, I saw it first—"

Their voices rose as we listened fascinated, wondering which of them wanted the table for a reason they weren't telling. None of us heard the footsteps in the hall or even looked up until Mrs. Travis and Miss Valentine stood in the doorway. But they, apparently, had heard everything.

"Sorry to disappoint you both," Miss Valentine said, smirking, "but you're too late. Mrs. Travis has already promised the table to me, and the chairs, too."

Ivy and Mr. Philips looked as if they wanted to say a really bad word. Miss Valentine's face reminded me of my cat's the time he trotted home with a steak from a neighbor's barbecue grill. Nothing could have shaken her then. Nothing except Susannah's next words.

"I don't think you *will* buy that table, Miss Valentine," Susannah said quietly. "Not unless you plan to pay—oh, I don't know, maybe ten thousand dollars. I'm not sure," she apologized, "exactly what a Croatian nobleman's two-hundred-year-old dining table is worth."

Miss Valentine sat down heavily on the nearest chair.

"Careful," Susannah warned. "That chair's valuable, too. It goes with the table, I think, along with others

scattered about the house—let's see, how many are in the picture?" As Mr. Philips snatched *Historical Mansions of Croatia* from her hands, she added, "The table is older than the picture, the caption says."

"But this is ridiculous!" burst out Ivy Withers. "All Uncle's antiques were stolen years ago."

Mrs. Travis laughed nervously. "Susannah, are you joking? You don't seriously believe that piece of junk is valuable?"

"This is the silliest thing I've ever heard." Miss Valentine made a disdainful face. "After all my years in the antique business, I should know one when I see one. That table isn't worth the thirty dollars I offered for it. As for this ghastly chair—"

Susannah barely spared her a glance. "It's time to prove our case. Mr. Philips, if we can have our chisel back—"

As we started toward the table, Miss Valentine jumped up angrily.

"Mrs. Travis, I won't have those little monsters tearing up that table I just bought."

Juliet answered, "You haven't bought it, Miss Valentine. It's mine, and I say they can do what they want to. Okay, Mom?"

Mrs. Travis met her eyes and nodded.

Mr. Philips handed us the chisel, and Knievel and I cautiously pried away a slat from the nearest leg. It came away easily, for it proved to be only thin plywood covered with wood-finish Con-Tact paper. Someone gasped at the first gleam of gold, and the next moment we were looking at an ornately gilded, curved leg. It was even more beautiful than it looked in the book and in the snapshot.

"But I don't understand," Ivy Withers half whispered. "I thought all Uncle's antiques were stolen."

"Yes, but the table and chairs arrived *after* the robbery." Susannah opened the secret drawer—the grownups murmured in surprise—and took a letter from the packet inside. "See, this letter from a New York shipper says they were sending some antique furniture to him. The date on the letter kept bothering me. Lucy, did you find out how long it takes to ship furniture from New York to California?"

"Oh," I said, realizing why I'd had that job. "A week or ten days maybe—usually longer."

"I thought so," said Susannah. "This letter's dated only two days before the robbery, so the stuff didn't arrive till afterwards. They couldn't deliver it anyway with nobody home, and Mr. Withers didn't get back until after the robbery."

Mr. Philips studied the letter. "John must have bought it in Europe, not knowing he was spending almost his last cent at the time. He didn't know he was ruined until he landed in New York."

"Anybody with a grain of sense would have sold a

thing like this in New York, not had it sent home to California, flat broke as he was," Ivy said sternly, but something seemed caught in her throat as she added, "Uncle hadn't a grain of sense."

"Not a grain," Mr. Philips agreed, with a hint of a smile. "But tell me, young lady"—he eyed Susannah respectfully—"how did you know?"

"The glue, for one thing," Susannah said. "There was glue on the rug—strong glue, the kind you use for wood. I looked around and noticed somebody had pried into the covering of the back leg of the table, then glued the pieces back. Whoever it was forgot this splinter, though."

Mr. Philips took the splinter from her and met Susannah's eyes. "You mean somebody knew about this table all along?"

By now Knievel and I had uncovered all four legs. The top, we discovered, was covered with a thick sheet of plywood, with more plywood added on the sides— all of it covered with the imitation-wood Con-Tact paper. Mr. Philips and Susannah helped us lift it off. Beneath the plywood was a quilted pad to protect the finish. When we slipped the pad away, even I sucked in my breath.

I'd never seen anything like it: the richly polished wood, the gracefully fluted sides, the heavy gilt carving at the corners.

Nobody seemed able to speak for a moment. It was Miss Valentine who broke the silence in a strange, raspy voice: "Has anybody got a light?"

I shouldn't have been surprised to see that she was holding a slim cigar.

Nineteen

I HAVE TO HAND IT to Miss Valentine, though. Her cool smile never wavered. Even when Susannah had removed the slipcover and foam rubber padding from the chair she'd planned to buy, Miss Valentine stared at the brocade underneath as if she'd never seen it before.

"Goodness me." She giggled unconvincingly. "You mean I nearly bought these priceless antiques by accident?"

Mrs. Travis didn't look amused. Neither did Mr. Philips. Even Ivy Withers frowned at her suspiciously.

"Well, I really must be running along," Miss Valentine said with a trace of nervousness. "But first let me congratulate you, dear." She squeezed Mrs. Travis' hand. "It couldn't happen to a nicer person. Oh, and I'll have my driver pick up that old bed and the other

153

junk for my cousin tomorrow. I'm sure a few extra dollars won't mean much now, but—"

Something stirred in my brain, but I was too dumbfounded to think. Were they just going to let this scheming woman walk out?

Mrs. Travis gave her a steely look. "To be frank, Miss Valentine, I don't wish to do business with you."

"Well!" Miss Valentine raised her plucked eyebrows to Ivy and Mr. Philips to witness such rudeness, but found no sympathy there.

"I don't suppose," Mr. Philips said acidly, "you also offered to buy a dozen or so other *ghastly* slipcovered chairs scattered around the house?" He glanced at Mrs. Travis, who nodded grimly. "Very interesting. Tell me, Miss Valentine, why would a dealer in fine antiques want so many junky-looking chairs?"

"I—I have several poor relations who need any kind of furniture," Miss Valentine blustered. She jerked her chin. "Are you accusing me? As a lawyer, you should know that's libel."

"Slander," Mr. Philips corrected. "But I haven't accused you . . . yet. I'm just wondering if the police will find fingerprints on that table and chair that match the ones you've left on your ashtray."

For a moment I thought she might make a grab for the ashtray, but instead she tossed her head. "Certainly my prints are on the table and chair. *All* of us were touching them a few minutes ago."

154

"True," Susannah spoke up. "I'm more curious to know if the cigar in your ashtray is the same brand as the one in a certain fishbowl in the junk room upstairs."

I knew as well as Susannah that there wasn't a trace of a brand left on the roll of ashes in the fishbowl. But I doubted that Miss Valentine was sure of that.

For the first time she looked shaken. "I don't know what you're talking about. Or what you're trying to prove. Surely you don't think I *knew* these things were valuable when I offered to buy them? How could I?"

"Because," said Susannah, "Mr. Withers told you, or dropped enough of a hint, that last day in the bus station."

Miss Valentine went so pale that her rouged cheeks stood out like strawberry jam on whipped cream. "I never—"

"Yes, you did," Susannah insisted. "The waitress saw you with him in the bus station. She identified you the other night at Miss Withers' party."

I felt like a fool. I should have realized that it was Miss Valentine, not Ivy, Jo recognized. For, of course, Jo didn't know which woman we'd taken her to see. But I was so sure it had to be Ivy talking with Mr. Withers in the bus station. I never even thought it might be the cost of repairing antiques, not the house, they were talking about. Of course, Jo's description of the woman should have tipped me off, as it did Susannah—"fancy," Jo called the way she was dressed. Ivy certainly wasn't a fancy dresser, but that was putting it mildly for the things Miss Valentine wore.

For a moment Miss Valentine seemed pinned to the end of Susannah's gaze. "When Mr. Withers died," Susannah said, her eyes firmly holding Miss Valentine's, "you started searching the house at night for the antiques you suspected must be hidden there. An ordinary burglar would have been fooled by what looked like junk, but not you. Something about this table caught your interest enough to chisel off a piece of plyboard covering the leg. It was careless of you," Susannah added reproachfully, "to spill glue on the rug while trying to glue the piece back."

But if we expected Miss Valentine to crumble and confess, we were disappointed. She pulled herself together and stalked to the door.

"I've listened to enough of your libelous—slanderous—insults. I'm going straight to my lawyer." And off she marched.

I crowed. "Boy, we've got her now! What'll they give her—fifty years in jail, you think?"

Mr. Philips smiled ruefully and shook his head. "It would be tough to prove anything. Even with fingerprints and that cigar stub you mentioned, and the waitress—"

"I'm afraid Jo's testimony wouldn't stand up in court," Susannah sighed. "She wasn't all that certain

156

about recognizing Miss Valentine since she's dyed her hair red. As for the cigar in the fishbowl, there's nothing left but ashes. I was just bluffing on a guess."

"You're a good guesser then, Sarah—no, Susannah, right?" Mr. Philips looked at her as if for the first time. "When you finish school and want a job, young lady, come see me first. Meanwhile," he turned to Mrs. Travis, "I don't advise you to prosecute Miss Valentine, but if you do, I'll be glad to give you any help I can."

Mrs. Travis smiled thanks but shook her head. "No, we've got the antiques she was after, and that's all we want. Right, honey?" She looked at Juliet, who nodded.

I couldn't stand it. "You mean you're just going to let that awful woman get away with it?"

Susannah squeezed my shoulder. "She'll get what's coming to her, Lucy, you'll see. When the story comes out in the newspapers, people are bound to wonder why an antique dealer was so anxious to buy junk that just happened to be valuable."

"They'll certainly get the story from me," Ivy said emphatically. "Believe me, dear, she's going to lose a lot of friends and customers."

I felt satisfied. At least, I would have if something off in a corner of my brain hadn't kept nudging me, like a job I'd forgotten to do. If only I could remember what.

"Lucy," said Susannah, as Mr. Philips marshaled everyone to go search for the missing chairs, "something's eating you. You've got that same funny look I saw on your face back awhile ago."

"Yeah," I said, realizing that something someone had said had jarred a piece of my memory. But what was it? All I could remember was Miss Valentine squeezing Mrs. Travis' unwilling hands. "Something Miss Valentine said . . . I can't remember. . . ."

"About wanting to buy the bed?" Susannah asked.

"The bed—yes, that's it! Susannah, there's a demon in that bed—I mean—oh, you mean you know?"

"I only know," said Susannah, "that it's interesting Miss Valentine wanted to buy a bed with a strange-looking lump in the headboard. I think it's high time we looked under the Con-Tact paper, don't you?"

Before I could reply, Susannah was bounding down the hall and up the stairs, Knievel right behind her with the toolbox, and the rest of us following. Crowding into the bedroom, we watched her jab the headboard with her finger and motion to Knievel.

"Give me something sharp."

Juliet sucked her breath as Susannah inserted the blade of Knievel's pocketknife into the covering of the headboard. There was a loud rip as it slashed through the Con-Tact paper and a layer of heavy fabric beneath. I squealed, for where the demon had been, an angel smiled out at us. A merry baby angel face,

carved into the polished wood of the headboard and lavishly covered in gold, perched on what was apparently a family crest.

Ivy Withers broke the silence. "Oh, my goodness!" she wheezed. "But why did Uncle cover up that magnificent headboard? He must have been crazy."

"No," said Susannah, carefully knifing away the covering from the intricately carved footboard. "Mr. Withers was just a practical man in his way. He knew nobody would steal a bed that looked like a piece of junk."

"Is it worth a lot?" Knievel asked hopefully.

"An awful lot, I'm betting," said Susannah. "I think it belonged to that Croatian count who owned the dining room stuff. See the crest under the angel? It's the same as the one over the doorway in one of the pictures. Hey"—she paused, staring over her glasses—"wonder if there's anything else of the count's here?"

For some reason Knievel and I both glanced at the bureau. "Uh-uh," I said. "It isn't even covered in Con-Tact paper or anything. It's just an old bureau with drawers that don't fit right."

Drawers! That pile of drawers in the junk room! I dashed down the hall behind Susannah, with Knievel and Juliet right after us. It didn't take long to find six drawers at the bottom of the pile, four large and two small ones, with gilded curlicues and angel faces on the handles and the count's crest in the middle. They

160

fit in the bureau perfectly, and what a different bureau it instantly became! That old count himself would have thought he was back home in his own bedroom in Croatia.

I won't bother telling you about our search for the eleven missing dining chairs, which was no search at all because Mrs. Travis remembered which ones Miss Valentine had offered to buy at three dollars each. Though Miss Valentine had made two mistakes: She'd apparently thought there were only ten chairs to the set, and two she had picked turned out to be nothing but unfinished kitchen chairs under the padding and slipcovers. Would she have been mad when she got them home! But we found the other four without much trouble. It was Ivy Withers who uncovered the last one, and we all cheered.

"Goodness, what a treasure hunt!" She laughed, easing herself down onto the chair she'd just found. "I haven't had so much adventure in years. No wonder Uncle didn't want my hand-me-downs. But"—her face puckered—"poor man, how could he enjoy these lovely things all covered up and looking so awful?"

I remembered the night I'd stood here in the dark and imagined the shadows of the junk furniture to be elegant antiques. Mr. Withers must have done that many a night.

"He knew they were here," I said. "He remembered how they really looked."

"And he could always take off their disguises and look at them whenever he wanted," Susannah pointed out. "The coverings slip off easily when you know how to do it, even the ones on the bed. He probably uncovered them often when he was alone, but covered them up again afterwards. It was the only way he knew to protect them from the robbers he feared above everything."

"No wonder," Juliet sighed. "He never got over that time everything was stolen."

"You suppose," Mr. Philips muttered, looking up from *Historical Mansions of Croatia*, "we've missed anything?" He addressed the question to Susannah.

"I'm wondering, too," said Susannah. "Ready for some more adventure, everybody?"

It was Knievel, I hate to admit, who noticed the rug in one of the pictures and remembered the faded carpet under the living room rug. Can you blame me for jeering at him? How was I to know that some Pittsburgh millionaire would later buy it for what it would probably cost to carpet a dozen houses?

If the Blue House held any more secrets, we never found them. Maybe somebody has since discovered another Croatian antique among the junk Mrs. Travis sold to a secondhand dealer after the museum and a San Francisco gallery bought the count's dining room and bedroom furniture, but I doubt it. If anyone did,

I just hope he or she deserved it as much as Juliet—who finally got her scar removed.

But that afternoon we were all too tired and hungry to think much about the future. Mrs. Travis invited us all to dinner. "It's the least I owe you," she said.

"No," Ivy Withers said firmly. "Let this be my treat. Uncle would like that, I think. I have a lot of questions about this whole puzzling business I want to ask this remarkable young lady." She nodded at Susannah.

We had to call our folks for permission. While Knievel and I wrestled for first turn at the telephone, Susannah slid past us and made her call. Then, seeing we might take all night to settle our argument, she got us to toss a coin.

Knievel won. Emptying his pockets, he brought out a scrap of paper stuck to a wad of bubble gum. As he dialed the number scribbled on it, I glanced at the paper.

I screamed. "Hey, that's *my* phone number!"

Knievel froze, his finger poised over the last number. "Can't be. That's where Mom said to call her tonight, at her friend Jim's."

Hearing Pop's name, my mouth went dry.

"Your mom"—I felt like a whole jar of peanut butter was stuck in my mouth—"her name isn't Mae . . . is it?"

Gazing at me in horror, Knievel nodded and let the receiver fall.

"Oh no!" we wheezed.

Susannah looked from one to the other of us and back. I could almost swear that behind her solemn face I caught a giggle.

"Well, partners," she said at last, "look at it this way: It will only take one phone call for both of you to get permission from your folks. So how about dialing the number, huh? I'm hungry."

PATRICIA ELMORE says: "Almost six years ago, while making a filmstrip on early childhood education, I saw a girl peering over her glasses at her work with such absorption that she barely glanced up at us as we photographed her. She caught my imagination so strongly that even after I'd persuaded our photographer to snap her, she kept interrupting all my carefully thought-out plots. Thinking about her as a character, I eventually realized she was a natural detective—and so plunged into my first effort at writing a mystery."

Ms. Elmore lives in Berkeley, California.

JOHN C. WALLNER enjoyed illustrating this book because it is a mystery, and also because "we had just bought a 150-year-old farmhouse that reminded me of the Blue House in the book—creaks and all."

He and his wife, also an illustrator of children's books, live in Woodstock, New York, with a dog and several cats. His most recent book is *Good Night to Annie* by Eve Merriam (Four Winds).